THE GREAT FLYING SAUCER INVASION

By
GEOFF ST. REYNARD

ARMCHAIR FICTION
PO Box 4369, Medford, Oregon 97504

For more information about Armchair Books and products, visit our website at…

www.armchairfiction.com

Or email us at…

armchairfiction@yahoo.com

IT WAS OVER IN ONE SWIFT BLOW...

When the flying saucers came to Earth it caused quite a stir. Panic and rioting was rampant. But then we were told that the aliens were just friendly explorers from outer space. After all, hadn't one of the alien pilots gone on national TV with the President? Hadn't he assured the world that his race—as alien as it might seem to Earth's peoples— had only the friendliest of intentions? The tall one-eyed green alien certainly looked friendly—outwardly at least.

And so it was. The United States government went out of its way to reassure its people (and the people of the world for that matter) that we had nothing to fear. We were told not to panic—everything was under control. But a veteran Army sergeant thought differently. He wasn't buying the whole "friendly explorer" thing. Little did he know that he was right. And then one day in early winter, the world was brought to its knees...

FOR A COMPLETE SECOND NOVEL, TURN TO PAGE 85

CAST OF CHARACTERS

TRACE ROSCOE
This tough Army sergeant was all about duty and loyalty, even if he thought the supreme commander-in-chief was dead wrong.

JANE KELLY
She wasn't your average weak female of the 1950s. And she was anything but weak when standing up to alien invaders.

BILL BLACKNIGHT
Little did he suspect that his skills as a magician would come in handy after the world had been stomped flat by alien invaders.

SLOUGH
He was just a little guy—almost a midget. But he seemed to have a quiet strength about him—or was it something more?

BARBARA SKYE
Definitely a looker—but her girlish charm and beauty seemed woefully out of place after the world came crashing down.

HAFNAGEL
Big and tough-looking, Roscoe needed him for his new "army." But it's funny what happens to people after their world is destroyed.

JOHNSON
He was a real sniveling coward, which begged the question…was he even worth saving?

CHAPTER ONE

DESPITE conflicting reports, the Air Force believed in the flying saucers. The scares began in 1947 and as a responsible agency the Air Force had to start investigations. At various times they'd cautiously release some information; then there would be some hysteria and they'd hurriedly debunk the whole business as "mass hallucinations" and "crackpot theories" until the public had regained its balance, then they'd start letting out bits of truth once more. The nature and implications of the saucer sightings made this on-again-off-again policy necessary in dealing with such an unstable thing as a war-nervous, tensed-up population. If the truth about the saucers had been known, the entire truth, then the Air Force could have published it and the country would have accepted it in stride; but the mystery that clouded the strange ships was susceptible of too many interpretations.

In December of 1952 a blue-lighted saucer was sighted, without a shadow of a doubt, over Laredo, Texas. In January of '53 a whole V-formation of blue objects appeared over Santa Ana, California. These were military sightings and beyond question. There were many before and even more afterward. Some of them mentioned blue lights and some other colors, and the daylight viewings talked of silver metallic luster.

The first low-flying saucer to be reported authoritatively was that which flew over the Capitol in Washington at 11:18 a.m. on Saturday, Christmas Day, 1954. It was caught by the cameras that were making a telecast at that time of the festivities in Washington, and beamed without explanation all over the country. A few minutes later the screens of America's viewers went blank and then the President appeared to urge calmness and sanity. There was no question of mass hallucination and crackpot theories any longer. The saucer was perhaps three hundred feet broad; it was of the usual shape reported in previous sightings, round with a central cabin, and it was green in color. It had flown comparatively slowly, at an estimated 125 m.p.h. It had disappeared over the Potomac.

At 2:24 p.m. the President was on TV again. There was some commotion at the door of the room from which he was broadcasting. He turned his head and nearly one hundred million people who were jammed before television sets across the nation saw his jaw drop and his eyes bulge slightly with irrepressible awe. In about nine seconds a very curious group walked into camera range. There were half a dozen secret service men with drawn guns, and in their midst, the target of those watchful weapons, was the first of the green horde.

He was—the measurements were determined later—six feet seven and one-half inches tall. He was dressed in a green shirt and trousers, caught around the waist by a heavy belt on which were stitched a number of cabalistic designs; on the left breast were more of the same, a circle and three slim triangles. In a holster slung at the right side of his belt was a large revolver or pistol. It was what had been known in the old West as a half-breed holster, enabling the wearer to swing up the muzzle and fire the gun without jerking it free of the leather. The alien had his hands folded carefully across his chest. Had he made a single motion toward the gun, he would have been blown in two.

In proportions and frame he was very like a human being. His chest was deep and his legs and arms well muscled. His skin was a delicate, olive-green in hue, as those viewers with color TV could see. His face was normal, perhaps a bit stern in expression, but with the ordinary features of a man, except that he had only one eye. It was located immediately above the bridge of his nose; it was about four times the area of a human eye and almost round in shape, and its small pupil roamed swiftly to and fro as the alien walked slowly toward the President. The pupil of the eye was like a tiny animal in a cage, dashing from side to side, up and down, uncanny, incredible, and horrifying.

THE cameras did not show his feet. These were somewhat like those of an ostrich, each having two enormous toes, naked, horny, and padded with thick layers of green fatty matter on the soles.

The tint of his skin could have been accepted as a mutation of the strictly human animal. The single eye, even, might have suggested a humanoid sport or far-future development. But the feet were utterly inhuman and even the most callous or most unimaginative among the citizens who saw him personally that first day agreed that the feet were terrifying.

The cameras were turned off after about twenty seconds. An announcer came on and spluttered some drivel about keeping cool and not losing our heads, spoiling the effect of these admonitions at once by a piercing, hysterical giggle.

Before a quarter of an hour had elapsed, there were minor riots and demonstrations throughout the continent. The worst of these were sparked by fanatic groups claiming that the end of the world had come. Others, scarcely less violent, went screaming that Martians were invading us, that the White House had been captured "right on the television" and much more of such idiocies. In many places militias were called out to suppress waves of looting and street fighting.

The Air Force, which had not been taken entirely unaware, since they had privately come to the conclusion some time before that the flying saucers were extraterrestrial, now flung a canopy of fighter planes, both jet and motor driven, over Washington. Somewhat later, Pittsburgh, Detroit, Birmingham and New York, Chicago, Los Angeles, and other cities of strategic importance were likewise protected—within a period of about two hours.

The rioting was subdued by evening. Army trucks equipped with public address systems patrolled everywhere, repeating the warnings to keep calm and do nothing until official word was broadcast of our intentions toward the aliens and vice versa. Meanwhile the first of the green horde was given a comfortable room in the Pentagon, where he was kept under an unobtrusive but thorough twenty-four-hour-a-day guard, and where means of communication with him were speedily sought for.

In a matter of a day and a half, or, to be precise, at two minutes to midnight on Sunday, the 26th of December, he articulated his first English word. It was "Yes." Shortly he proved that he had absorbed much more than this word, for he began making attempts at complete sentences around 2:00 a.m. on the 27th. He had been under the constant supervision and teaching of a corps of scientists, language experts, and assorted brain-workers; he had shown no desire for sleep during the thirty-six hours he had been on the ground, and had listened to and worked with the teachers all that time. He showed now a good rudimentary grasp of English. It was given as the official opinion that he had shown in this the intelligence of a human genius, although not of the very highest order, rating perhaps an IQ of 195.

IN THE eight-hour period following this he spoke with the President and assured him, partly in words and partly in signs, that the folk of the green saucers were friendly explorers from a distant galaxy. His voice was throaty and rather unpleasant, with a tendency to crack in the upper registers.

He expressed a desire to return to his saucer for some purpose, which he could not make plain with his basic English. This was at 10:17 a.m. on the 27th. It was considered diplomatic to allow him to enter the saucer alone. He did so by a method that was, unfortunately, not communicated to the public later. Shortly the craft rose from the earth and shot rapidly out of sight in the direction of Mount Vernon. There was no jet exhaust detected in its takeoff; it simply rose like an iron filing to a magnet, soundless and abrupt. For three days thereafter there were no reported sightings of saucers.

It was officially decided in this period that the green man with the single eye and bird's feet was not intent on mischief; he had been given an idea of how far we had progressed technically, in many fields, but the information was only what he and his kind could have discovered for themselves in the years-long surveillance of Earth. No secrets had been imparted to him and he had expressed nothing but cordiality and good will, though he had managed to tell the interrogators only a little about himself and his race and home planet, which when boiled down and analyzed came to this: his home was far away (of course it would be) and he was friendly.

After the three-day lapse, saucers were detected on radar screens all over the civilized world—rather too high for the usual reconnaissance, they came and passed in greater numbers than ever before. No planes reported them, their altitude being too great. This long-distance saucer traffic worried the governments of every nation. It was capable of so many explanations that deduction was futile. The protective canopies of fighter planes remained over key cities in the United States and Canada, and to some extent over the capitals and industrial centers of the world.

Eight days after the tremendous influx of saucers, Russia issued her considered opinion. "The green one-eyed man was a capitalistic hoax. No such creature existed. The radar blips were "a" natural phenomenon, "b" a secret weapon of the Soviet, "c" a secret weapon of America and or Britain, or "d" a capitalistic hoax. Somehow the masters of propaganda made it appear that all four of these silly charges were true, notwithstanding their mutual cancellation.

Two days thereafter the green horde launched its attack, at 11:34 a.m. on Sunday, the 9th of January, 1955.

CHAPTER TWO

ALTHOUGH the great flights of fighter planes were continually aloft, the reassuring program had gone on, the broadcasting trucks still rumbling about the streets foghorning their messages of cheer and optimism to a somewhat restive public. Some elements of the free press had been warning direly of "unknown dangers" and "possible treachery, this causing some gimlet-eyed gentlemen in high places to come out with bills and demands for suppression of a free press for the duration of the so-called negotiations with the alien people. There had been no negotiations whatever. In this case, as in many others, the free press was perfectly right; but their warnings in the face of official hopefulness served only to confuse and fret the public. Hence, the TV lulled, the radio allayed, and the bellowing loudspeakers on the cruising trucks attempted to quiet fear under a blanket of sound.

At the said moment of attack, 11:34 a.m., the green saucers swept down with a perfection of simultaneity that made you think, as someone said later, that the devil had murmured, "Synchronize your watches, boys." They hurtled from the skies over New York and Bangkok and Berlin and London and Madrid and Shanghai, down upon Moscow and San Francisco and Tokyo and Paris and Bombay. In the instant that the devastation hit New Orleans it also smashed at Edinburgh and Nome and Minsk and Berne. The first skyscraper toppled in Chicago as the first factory blew to smithereens in Rio de Janeiro.

It was curious that their weapons did not seem to include the atomic variety. No A-bombs or H-bombs; rather, it was rays—rays of incalculable destructive power and unknown origin. They lanced from the diving saucers and struck the earth with the force of exploding bombs; but instead of crashing and then echoing away, these explosions continued, like great rolls of terrible thunder, for as long as the rays were aimed downward. One ray, directed from the belly-port of a canting ship would set the ground a-shudder, crumple all structures in its path or near it, and create an ear-shattering blast that kept on and on until the saucer, tilting away, shut off the ray. So that each ray, in effect, was like an unending and ever-replenished series of huge bombs—and from each ship came a ray, and over each city there were hundreds of ships...

The mighty centers of civilization were obliterated. The great concentrations of population over the globe died. Manufacturing cities and cities that produced nothing of strategic value whatever were smeared indiscriminately into blood and dust and muck. It was an attack, not at man's weapons or production, but at man himself. It was the beginning of man's end, a giant step toward his classification with the dodo, the auk, the saber-tooth tiger and the passenger pigeon.

One large eastern city in the United States presented a typical picture during that hour of cataclysm. In the first fifteen minutes its canopy of fighter planes was blown out of the sky; the weapons they carried, some of them atomic, were as effective against the green saucers as slingshots on platinum. By noon the air had begun to fill with billowing, drifting masses of smoke-yellow vapor, reeking of sulfur and molten metal and burnt flesh and death. Those who had been unlucky enough to live through the attack thus far were now so nauseated by the odors of mankind's collapse that they stumbled among the shattering streets, retching and vomiting, as eager to escape the yellow hell-cloud's stink as they were to avoid the crumbling steel and cement.

AT the end of an hour, while the greater part of the two hundred and twenty-eight saucers continued to raze the city, one alien ship made a landing on a leveled field of the suburbs. Its entry port jawed open, somewhat like a huge clamshell parting, and a single green man emerged. He was six feet nine and his eye measured a good four inches across. He carried a flag of red, white and green, on which the device of a circle, and three triangles, which he wore on his left breast, was repeated. He strode away from the ship, gazing about with satisfaction. Some distance off lay the wreckage of a broadcasting truck; its warped, ruined loudspeakers yawned over the body of an Army sergeant, who still held in a firm grip the microphone into which he had been talking when the world was scuttled around him.

On the side of the demolished truck there remained a sign drenched in irony, which read DON'T PANIC—THEY'RE FRIENDLY!

There was blood on the sergeant's mouth and forehead and he had bled from the nose. The blood was almost wholly dry now. His eyes were open.

The green conqueror looked at him and grinned. It remains one of the most curious facts of the matter that both mankind and the bird-footed beasts of the green horde expressed amusement and pleasure by turning up the corners of the mouth...

The alien peered all about him, shading his eye with his right hand. Nothing moved anywhere except the skimming saucers and the collapsing city. He stepped forward and lifted his pennon high, to plant its ten-foot staff in the dead body of the Earthman. Holding it up, he spoke a few words in his own language, a guttural cracking speech that ranged up and down like that of an excited bird.

As he was about to stab the corpse with his flag, the corpse rolled onto its back and contracted its body, shot up its feet and kicked the alien square in the belly.

Catching the shaft of the flag, the erstwhile dead sergeant jerked it out of the alien's grasp, immediately bounded to his feet, took a firm two-handed grip of the thing—the sharp lance-head made it a splendid weapon— and ran it with savage violence straight into the throat of the green man, who died instantly and without sound.

Pausing only to shake his head once, because it ached fiercely, the sergeant bent over the tall body, folded one big hand around the pistol and its half-breed holster, and yanked. The retaining strap broke. The sergeant turned and began to run in the opposite direction from the grounded saucer, which continued to show no sign of life. Shortly he had disappeared into the smoking, burning ruins of the city's edge.

And so at 12:46 p.m. on January 9th, 1955, a moribund world drew the first blood from its extraterrestrial assassins.

CHAPTER THREE

TRACE Roscoe had been a sergeant, off and on, for nine years. He belonged to the regular Army and had never thought of choosing any other career. Twice he had been busted to corporal and twice regained his stripes. Once he had been up for a commission and had, after due thought, refused it, because he'd known he wouldn't have it long. He had an Irish temper, and that was from his mother; he had a bulldog English muddle-through determination, and that was from his father. He was a hell of a good man in a fight. He was the best driver in his company, a better mechanic than a driver, and a better boxer than either. He read adventure novels and Von Clausewitz and Spillane and Voltaire and anything else that happened his way. He didn't consider himself much of a brain, but would have smeared the man who implied he was less intelligent than Einstein, for a man's opinion of himself should not be held by other people.

He had been driving his broadcasting truck along Highwood Avenue when the saucers attacked. He had been reciting the rhetoric about not panicking, and hoping that he could personally see one of the single-eyed aliens sometime. He put no faith in the friendly-explorer crud. He wanted to look into that lone eye and decide for himself what the critters intended, because Trace Roscoe fancied himself a pretty good judge of character, even the character of ostrich-hoofed schmoes from outer space.

Well, the earth rose up around him and his truck before he rightly knew what was going on, and after a period of blackness he woke up to pain and a stench like one of Poe's charnel houses in his nostrils. He found that he was lying with his left arm draped over a jagged hunk of truck, clutching the mike with stiff fingers. Not being one to act without thinking in an emergency, he lay perfectly quiet and listened for a while to the rumble and crump of bombs—which he later found out had been the rays from the saucers instead—and the buzzing of his own skull. He could taste blood and feel it drying on his skin. He didn't believe he was at all badly hurt.

A little way from his face there was a busted headlight. He gazed at it a while, collecting his thoughts and opinions, and noticing that an arrangement of the shattered glass and chrome made a quite respectable mirror in which he could see a good deal of what went on behind him. Before he had decided what to do, he saw the saucer come to ground on the blasted field. He played possum and after a bit he saw the greenie come up the rise and stand there glaring around, holding the queer pennon and tipping back the pronged helmet from his eye.

Trace concentrated on holding still until the critter stepped over to him, and then Trace exploded all over the poor bastard, and took away his gun, which he wouldn't be needing any longer, and ran.

He half expected to be popped off by a bullet or a ray or a lord-knew-what from the saucer, but he reached the first edge of ruins safely and went to ground like a rabbit. Sitting in an angle of broken wall, he scanned the city. The saucers were engaged in a final mop-up. Trace felt sick. He looked at his town from end to end and he knew there couldn't be a dozen people alive in it. He had no way of knowing what was happening to the rest of the world, but he made some shrewd guesses. He was aware of the incredible number of blips that had been showing up on the radar screens lately. He knew that this city wasn't important enough in the scheme of things to warrant more than a small section of the attacking forces. This must be what Revelations called "the great day of God" when good and evil fought it out at Armageddon. Except that evil seemed to be winning, hands down.

TRACE Roscoe peeked over his wall at the grounded saucer, and saw that a lot of greenies were coming out of it, advancing cautiously toward their dead comrade who lay with ten feet of flagpole sticking up from his throat. Trace counted them as an automatic action (there were seventeen), in case he would need to know how many made up a saucer's crew in the future. Then he bent low and ran from hillock to hillock through what had that morning been the southwestern suburbs of his city. As he ran he discarded the holster of the alien's gun, and thrust the weapon itself into his belt. If he had had a few minutes to examine it, and had he discovered how many loads it carried, he would have remained and started a fight with the one-eyers. Running was strategically correct in view of his ignorance of his only weapon.

When he had covered a mile he got up on a one-story-high mound of rubble and looked back. The green men had planted their flag and returned to their craft; even as Trace watched, it rose like a round green bullet and disappeared above the yellow haze. None of the other saucers landed, so far as he could see. The landing, then, had been for the vain, glorious purpose of leaving their banner in token of victory. Trace spat and jumped down and went on into the city.

The reek made him gag now and then, but he had smelled some truly awful things in his time and was able to control his uneasy stomach. He considered the possibility of poison gas and judged it too slight to worry over; the destroying rays had certainly no need of accompanying gases, for they were as all-destructive as a thousand hurricanes rolled up in one package.

By three o'clock (his watch, miraculously, was still going) Trace had entered the city itself. He trotted down a broken, heaped-up thoroughfare, his glance roving constantly from side to side in search of movement. A sergeant whose army was gone had to find himself another in a hurry; and if he was to be the general in that one, well, Trace Roscoe was ready to take on the job.

He had no fanatical hope of beating the greenies, because he was a soldier and levelheaded, and odds of some millions to one were no odds at all. He figured the enemy's strength at something between ten and a hundred thousand saucers, with at least twenty individuals crewing each. There were, at a conservative estimate, 200,000 troops on the other side; and possibly more like 2,000,000. So Trace was not indulging in any optimism when he started hunting for an army. He was merely following his natural inclination, which was to fight the opposition as long as he had breath in his body and hands on the ends of his arms.

He was not full of sorrow and wild regret either, for that wasn't Trace's way. Besides which, the destruction of the civilization of Earth was too big to be grasped and understood all at once. If Trace had found the bodies of a score of people, he might have burst into tears, for his heart was big and Irish and sentimental. But pacing down the stinking tomb of hundreds of thousands of men and women was so incredible as to be simply a fact and not a comprehendible horror.

Alone he stood in the middle of a more-or-less flat plain in the city, staring and listening; and when he heard the shout, he went toward it at once, exulting that so quickly he'd discovered a private, or it might be a captain, for his army. There was a hole that was floored with cracked steps and went down into the ground, and Trace dived into it without hesitation.

SITTING at the bottom, with chunks of concrete heaped around him like divot around a duffer's tee, was a thin gentleman in a mustache, half a top hat, one leg of a pair of black trousers, and little else but a scowl. "They killed her," he said as Trace came into his view. "They blew her right out of my arms."

"Can you stand?" Trace asked him, reaching out one big hand.

"I don't know. Ouch! Yes, I can," said the man. "I tell you, they murdered Fannie."

"I'm sorry, fellow. Your wife?"

"My rabbit."

"Rabbit?" Trace turned him around and looked him over for wounds; there were none more serious than extensive bruises.

"I'm a magician," said the naked man. "Blacknight the Great. I had Fannie for three years and she never made a mistake. Smartest damn rabbit you ever saw. I was carrying her to a shelter and one of those rays shot along over the Farinello Building and the whole street blew up and she was gone, just like that. Damn green monsters."

He stared at the sergeant. "I suppose it seems silly to you, feeling bad about a rabbit?"

"No," Trace said shortly. "I had a marmoset once. Let's get out of here and see how many others are alive."

"I haven't heard a thing for an hour," Blacknight said. "Not until your footsteps in the gravel. I think they're all gone." The two men stood in the open, craning their necks. "Nobody," the thin man said bitterly. "Two men left out of a world. We can't even start our race again. That takes a female too," he said suddenly, and put his hands over his face.

"Come on," Trace Roscoe said sharply. "I'm hungry."

The naked magician looked up at him. "In the middle of this?" he said, and then, considering, "I guess I am too. I wouldn't have thought it was possible."

Farther along they found the remains of a two-story department store; a lot of it was gone, but in the mess they managed to find a shirt and a pair of pants for Bill Blacknight—he swore it was his own name—and a couple of cans of corned beef hash. They invented a skillet and stove out of twisted metal, and shortly had wolfed down the hash and were prowling further into the city.

Trace saw the policeman first. He was walking in a tight little circle around a shattered telephone pole, waving his revolver and talking loudly to nobody. Trace sneaked up within a dozen yards before the cop spotted him. The first bullet cut his ear and the second missed, and then Trace had the gun. He tried to subdue the policeman but the poor devil was hopelessly mad. Trace shot him mercifully in the head. He took the cartridges out of the leather belt and dropped them into his shirt pocket and stuck the gun beside the alien's weapon in his belt. He and Bill

Blacknight traveled on, going methodically from street to street in search of recruits.

WHEN dusk came they had six more people. Bill told Trace that it was the damn silliest-looking excuse for an army than he could imagine. Trace shrugged. "They're human, anyhow."

"Are you sure?" Bill asked him. "Even Slough?"

"He has two eyes," said Trace, "and that's the only qualification a man needs for my army."

Slough might be called a midget. He stood exactly four feet high. He was beautifully proportioned, smoothly muscled and lithe-looking. He had a large head with a wild mane of yellow hair, and his eyes were pure Delft blue. He spoke in professorial tones and appeared entirely unaffected by the fact that his left arm was broken below the elbow. Trace set it for him, expertly and swiftly, while Slough talked quietly and with six-syllable words of the ghastly doom he hoped to see visited on the alien destroyers. He said he had been an airplane designer. He was without doubt the most intellectual member of Trace Roscoe's forces, and the only one save Bill Blacknight the magician whom Trace felt he could trust.

There were two girls, redheaded Barbara Skye who had been a secretary and couldn't seem to stop saying how awful, how awful it all was; and a dark-haired woman of twenty-five or so, who had not said a word thus far. Trace believed she was sane, but stunned into a sort of walking coma. He did not therefore consider killing her in mercy, but took her along as a potential ally.

The other three men, all office workers, looked useless; but Trace was setting out to avenge his world, and he had to accept every scrap of manpower that came his way. The three were in various degrees of shock, the worst being Johnson, who wept and shivered if you looked at him, the next Kinkaid, a plump balding man with a bad case of shudders who kept trying to run away from the little band, and the best Hafnagel, almost as big as Trace, with a tic in his cheek and fingers so rigid with nerves as to be almost useless. Johnson had had a rifle when they found him, a heavy sporting thing with four loads that he'd picked up in the rubble of a firearms shop. Trace had taken it from him and given it to Bill Blacknight. Johnson had been too frightened and sick to protest.

Trace sat them down in a circle on the highest point of what had been the city, where tumbled buildings and upheaved earth made a barren hill that would never produce anything, flowers or homes, for a thousand years... He stood among them and began to talk. His manner was that of a sergeant with a detail of raw recruits.

"Okay. There are seven of you and by and large I've seen better material, but you'll have to do. Now I'll tell you what we're going to do. We're going to find the green lice that did this to our country, and blast 'em. We're going to make 'em wish they'd never left Venus, or Mars, or wherever the hell they sprang from."

Hafnagel, the big man with stiff hands, said something unprintable. "How are we going to do that, you big jerk? How can you fight a flying saucer?"

TRACE gave him a look that in its time had crackled the enamel on the teeth of many a GI. He said slowly, "My name is Sergeant Roscoe and I am your commanding officer and you had better remember it, Mac, or you will have cause to wish you had become extinct some years before you ever laid eyes on me. Now I shall continue.

The fleet of enemy ships left here at a terrific pace between one and two o'clock this afternoon, heading in the direction of Washington, D.C. I haven't spotted one since. Therefore what we will do is pick up our flat feet and head for the capital. God knows what we'll find there, but it's a cinch we've got to get out of here plenty fast."

"Why?" asked Kinkaid, the fat one.

"For one thing, Mac, they'll not be back this way, because what have they got to come back for?" asked Trace patiently.

"All the more reason to sit right here," said Hafnagel. "We can dig enough out of the ruins to live like kings."

"Ignoring the fact that you are gonna go where I say you're gonna go," said Trace through his teeth, "let me ask you, Mac, to take a sniff of the breeze."

"The smell's bearable."

"It will get worse. By this time two days from now it'll be enough to suck the guts out of you. I needn't say why."

"Oh," said Hafnagel, his cheek twitching. "Oh, I hadn't thought—"

"Exactly. Don't try to. Just listen to me. I am your superior officer, Mac," said Trace, "and with you and these other slewfooted remnants I am going to put a crimp in them Martians—*those* Martians—that they'll feel clean to the GHQ. Now we'll take ten and be on our way. I want to clear this area before the atmosphere gets serious."

He looked at them, seven shivering people huddled from the cold into the coats, scarves and parkas they had managed to snatch before their universe had erupted into nothingness. Despair was unknown to Trace Roscoe, but a grin of wonder touched his mouth; wonder at his own temerity. He was leading these poor reluctant untrained slobs against a million or two giant bird-footed interplanetary warriors, and with about nine-tenths of his mind he expected to do some damage to them. The other tenth said to him, with the voice of his grandmother, "Och, Trace boy, it's mad you are, mad clean through to your Irish bones."

"Wirra, Grandmother," Trace said to her in his head, "it's the bloody English in me too, d'ye see, that won't let me stop sluggin' and won't admit I can be whupped; and then there's all the American of me, and ye know fine that an American never is whupped at all—at all!"

He chuckled—first time that day—and sat down to examine the alien's pistol by the flare of his lighter.

CHAPTER FOUR

THERE was a good-enough moon. They made the outskirts of the city by eleven o'clock. A restaurant, all but demolished, gave them canned food; Trace had to bat Johnson in the chops to keep him from wolfing down a dirty chicken sandwich he found lying on the floor, and Johnson went into a fit of wailing hysterics, but when he came out of it he was just about cured, and didn't weep or shiver any longer. They walked a little farther and at midnight Trace plunked them down on a wooded hill, beyond the rayed area. He and Bill Blacknight gathered dry brush and built a blazing fire against the chill of January.

"Dangerous?" queried Slough, the tiny man.

"Calculated risk," said Trace. "I think we can presume the saucers won't be over this sector for a while, and if they do come, they may believe it's a natural fire. The main reason is to attract survivors to us." He didn't mention that he himself was so inured to climatic changes he would never have thought of building a fire for warmth, save for the others. He wore his heavy shirt and trousers and over them a light topcoat Bill had found for him. He could not have said off-hand whether he was cold or comfortable.

When they had all gone to sleep, some like corpses and others as light-slumbering as wildcats, Trace walked a beat around them, keeping an eye and an ear open for approaching steps. There were none.

Toward morning he heard the dark girl sobbing. He sat beside her and stroked her hair soothingly. When Bill took the watch, Trace fell asleep with one arm over the girl's shoulders. At dawn she was all right, and could talk again.

Her name was Jane Kelly and she'd been a teacher, and Trace considered her a very fine-looking dish indeed, even in the fat parka. She was not so flamboyantly female as Barbara Skye, the redhead, but she was distinctly not the sort you would take for a boy at forty paces. She had curves and a warm face and eyes like brown gold, if there was such a thing.

TRACE SAID, "Yo," like John Wayne was always doing in those Old West pictures about the cavalry. "Let's travel." The whole group of them rose and tramped off toward Washington.

They never reached it. They never even got as far as Philadelphia.

The first trouble came as they were crossing a field of frozen mud and corn stalk stubble; Barbara turned her ankle and sat down with a squawk. She was wearing high heels, not spikes but a good two-and-a-half inches, and Trace was disgusted with himself for neglecting his job. He was so full of vengeance and hatred that he forgot to check on the little things that could sabotage him. He should have scrounged some shoes for her somewhere yesterday.

He glanced at Jane's feet. She wore sensible shoes. They didn't improve her ankles any, but they couldn't spoil them either. Trace had never been an admirer of sensible shoes, yet now he felt a rush of affectionate gratitude to Jane for wearing them.

"You can't go barefoot," he said to Barbara, who was chattering petulantly and rubbing her ankle, exposing an astonishing length of silken thigh in the process. "And you can't travel in those things. You'll have to be carried."

"Why don't you leave her?" said Kinkaid, the plump man. "She's no use to you. Neither am I. I'll stay with her."

Barbara said venomously, "I'd as soon be stranded with one of those bird-footed weirdies as with you, Tubby. Take your cotton-pickin' eyeballs off my leg before I scratch them out for you."

Hafnagel, the big man, said, "Take a vote, Roscoe. You can't force us to limp all over creation with you. Because you're crazy enough to want to find the saucers is no—"

"I'm no soldier," said Johnson. He was a blond man with a crooked nose and jug-handle ears. "I'm going to take to the hills. The aliens are invincible; but a man might avoid them for years in the hills. There's farms and such to live off."

"Don't think I'll go with you," said Barbara, standing up. "I wouldn't trust one of you creeps if Roscoe was out o' sight. I'm going with him if I have to walk on my palms."

"We're not splitting up," said Trace. "Someone's got to carry you, honey." His breath misted out on the frosty air. "Hafnagel, you're big enough."

Hafnagel knelt down. Barbara straddled his shoulders, the man took her ankles carefully in his stiff fingers, as impersonally as if they had been firewood, rose and started forward. "Hey," Barbara said, "this is okay. You can see from up here."

"Any saucers?" asked Trace.

"No. Nothing moving at all." They all went on.

Trace's troubles multiplied through the day. Of all his crew, only three were interested in cracking back at the destroyers—the midget Slough, the magician Blacknight, and the teacher Jane Kelly. Barbara was against his plan, but would not leave Trace, whose uniform gave her a sense of security. The three others fought him constantly, with words and sometimes with action.

Hafnagel tried to knock him out during a halt. Trace presented him with a bloody nose, and saddled him with Barbara and drove them all onward.

Johnson broke for cover when they passed a willow-bordered river. Trace caught up with him and washed his face in the icy current, and Johnson restricted himself to verbal attacks thereafter.

Kinkaid refused to budge from their noon camp. Trace grabbed his left ankle and dragged him over the hard rocky earth for twenty yards, and Kinkaid shrieked that he'd walk. Later he pretended to go lame, fooled Trace into half-carrying him for a mile, and then had his fat face slapped so hard that he was filled with respect for Trace's authority, and made no more trouble.

THOSE were the intentional oppositions. Trace had likewise to contend with recurrent hysterics, with terrible fits of moaning agony of mind, and with a depression that now and again settled over the entire company. He bellowed at them, shoved them around, occasionally patted them like dogs; he realized what they were going through, and he was not a callous man, but he knew he had to keep them on the move for their own sakes as well as that of his plan. Civilization had all but died yesterday. He couldn't expect to pick up a gang of hard, angry, levelheaded companions. He had to make do with what he had, and improve on this weak raw material by his tough, high-handed methods.

Again and again he examined the strange firearm he'd taken from that green beast with the flag. It baffled him. There was no place to load the thing, no jointure in all its smooth dark surface. The muzzle was pierced by a hole about a millimeter wide. That was where the missile would come out; but could the weapon be reloaded there? What kind of ammo would go into a millimeter opening?

The pistol—he deeded to call it that—was much lighter than a Colt of comparable size. There was a narrow trigger and bigger guard in the same position as on an earth-made revolver. That was logical, as the hands of the aliens were, barring the color, perfectly human. Trace decided he'd have to take a chance and fire the thing. The unchancy weapon would come in handy if he could work it. He bit his lip. Maybe it had just one shot. Oh, blazes. He had to find out.

On their next halt, he aimed it at a tree (there was no sight and he aimed by feel, like a gunman) and pulled the trigger. It had a hard pull, so hard that only a strong man could have budged it at all. It made no sound. There was a thin streak of green light, and the trunk of the tree commenced to smoke and steam. Then it burst into yellow-green flame and exploded, fragments of bark and splintered wood showering out to a great distance. Trace ducked, let up on the trigger, and the beam died. He was reasonably sure now that it wasn't a one-shot.

"And that's what you want us to go against," said Johnson. "A million Martians armed with those. What right have you to make us?" he shrieked. "What authority?"

"This authority," said Trace, hefting the pistol. "Likewise the supreme authority of the United States Army, as I have declared martial law. And then there's the authority of me, Sergeant Trace Roscoe, who will mop up this whole damn valley with your fat puss if so be it you are disinclined to obey my orders, buster."

"Thinks he's so tough," grumbled Kinkaid.

But they all followed Trace when he marched on. Jane Kelly kept up easily with the men, and Trace was especially proud of her; but he had to admit that most all of them were whipping into shape better than he'd any right to hope for. "Few more days and I'll have me a real fine belly-achin' fighting-mad platoon here," he said to himself.

Unfortunately he didn't have a few more days. He made contact with the green-skinned destroyers no more than half an hour thereafter.

CHAPTER FIVE

THEY lay on the crest of a hill. Before them was a rolling plain spotted with patches of old snow. A thousand yards from the base of the hill was a small town, with figures moving among the houses. It had not been blasted by the saucers, but Trace's people did not run down the slope toward it, because along that plain from horizon to horizon rested a line of the great green spacecraft; and the moving figures, there was little doubt, had olive skin and horny bird-feet and a single eye apiece.

"Reconnoiter," breathed Trace. "Got to know what's what. That place must be local GHQ, and they look dug in pretty solid. I'm going down after dark and give 'em a squint. I'll take Bill with me, in case I want to bring back souvenirs."

"I'm rather more insignificant in the dark, than he," said Slough quietly. "And you ought to have three on the party."

"Your arm would slow you down."

"It would not," said Slough firmly. Trace looked at him and after a moment shrugged. "You're right, I could use another." He took the sporting rifle from Bill and gave it to Jane Kelly. He offered the revolver to Slough, who refused it; he handed it to Bill, keeping the alien's pistol for himself. Then he drew the teacher off a short distance. "Look, miss," he said earnestly, "I want you to keep these inter-office-memo types waiting here for me if you can. I don't expect you to actually shoot 'em, but maybe the rifle will cow 'em some. They aren't what you'd call blood and guts sort."

"Why don't you let them go?" she asked suddenly. "What good will three cowards do for you?"

"You never know, I figure they are human, and in the long run they'll show it. Hafnagel is the best—if he has time to recover. He lost his wife in the city."

Jane said, "I was lucky. I hadn't anyone to lose. Except mankind."

Trace looked at her steadily. "At another time, Miss Kelly," he said, "I'd like to tell you what a hell of a fine female you are. I know it wouldn't mean anything to you now, but I must say you are one swell dish." Then he blushed all over his big hawk-nosed face, and turned abruptly to the saucer-cut plain.

In the first darkness the three of them crawled over the top and headed down the slope.

THE greenies kept no guard of any kind on their headquarters town; nor, so far as Trace could see, did they set a sentinel over their saucers. They were horribly sure of themselves, sure of having crushed the highest race on this planet. The night was nearly black, thick jetty clouds obscuring the moon, and stabs and splashes of orange light showed where the aliens walked. The three Earthmen made their way to the edge of town, took a road straight toward the center, and trotted down the sidewalk past silent houses. They were cautious, but even so they nearly ran into a greenie who came round a corner, not twenty yards ahead. They went to earth under a hedge and watched him walk by. The orange illumination was explained: from the front of the helmet he wore, a beam of strong undiffused, red-yellow light shot out and down, showing him the path as he walked with bent head. Luckily he did not flick it from side to side, or he must have seen them crammed under the hedge.

When his soft padding footsteps had died, the midget Slough said urgently, "Trace, do you intend capturing one?"

"I might at that. Why?"

"If you do, remove his helmet at once. Immediately!" His breath mingled frostily with Bill's and Trace's. "The triple prongs atop the helmet may be antennae, for radiating and receiving waves, either of thought or a form of radio. It may be thus that they communicate, so knock off the helmet at once if you attempt a capture, or if we're discovered."

"You are a shrewd cookie," said Trace thoughtfully. "Okay, will do, now let's get the lead out."

The town had been a small place, with one drug store, one theater, half a dozen stores. The men prowled all round the heart of it, and Trace said, "Here's something funny. They haven't shown any curiosity. The theater's still locked up tight, like it must have been on Sunday when the attack was made on the cities. How come? Don't they want to check on what a building like this is used for? They don't seem to have pried into much of anything."

"Maybe they're not interested in us," said Bill. "Maybe they don't give a whoop for what we've done and how we've progressed. What if they considered themselves so superior to us that they thought we had nothing to teach them? Then they wouldn't pry into our heritage and culture. They'd just obliterate us."

"And why bother to obliterate us?" asked Slough.

"Lot of answers to that," said Trace briefly. "Meanness, desire for sense of power, what have you. Let's nail one and drag tail." He led them past the movie house, and gestured at an orange light approaching. "That one."

"Don't forget the helmet," urged Slough.

"Take it easy, Mac," said Trace huskily. They went to ground behind evergreen shrubs on the lawn of a funeral parlor.

The tall creature neared them, his horny feet with their heavy pads making little noise on the cement. He passed, and Trace launched himself at the broad back, feeling joy wash through him in a heady wave at the first action since his attack on the flag-planter. He struck the alien with all the weight and power of his two hundred pounds, expecting it to pitch forward on its face. It did nothing of the sort. It staggered one step, stiffened, and whirled on him. He clutched wildly for a grip, but the stonewall character of this great beast had thrown off his timing. The thing hit him in the face with a forearm. Trace reeled back and fell into a pine tree.

BILL Blacknight leaped on the one-eye even as Trace was hurled away, and darting up one long arm, the magician hit the helmet with the tips of his fingers. In a flash the dexterous hand found the edge of the metal and flipped upward. The alien, squawking, reached for the headgear, just too late. It clanged on the sidewalk. Bill wrapped himself around the steel-tough torso. He knew nothing of brawling, but he was as slippery as an oiled eel. The green man groped for him and he was somewhere else. Terrible hands groped to tear his head from his body, and Bill was a human cummerbund, folded around the waist of the thing and punching desperately for a vulnerable spot. Then he had flattened up along its back and had a half nelson on the thick throat.

The greenie drew his weapon. Bill did a contortionist trick and booted it out of his hand.

Trace climbed out of the pine tree, swearing bluely.

Slough appeared before the alien, who tensed his arms to grip the tiny man. Slough was no more than three feet away, well within reach and full in the glare of the fallen helmet's lamp; yet the one-eyed marauder did not catch him. Bill had forced him to his knees. The huge round eye glared across at Slough, while the thing appeared to wait for something unguessable to happen. Slough swung his good arm and caught the brute a healthy crack on the jaw. With a bird's cry, high and ferocious, like the wail of an eagle that has sighted on a rabbit and seen it turn into a wolf, the greenie jerked his head back and staggered to his two-toed feet.

Trace came in like Joe Louis at Tony Galento. He put a fist into the rigid belly and it smashed in like so much well chewed bubble gum. Then he pasted the alien in the throat, pulling his punch just enough so as not to shove the spine through the nape of the neck. Last, as the alien was toppling over, he unleashed the left uppercut that had won him seventy bouts in two years. The greenie flipped up his face and stared sightlessly at the black sky for an instant, whereafter he crumpled into a heap that would never get up and walk away under its own power if it lay there till the crack of doom.

The three friends panted a little at each other.

"Swell captive you have there," said Bill at last. "A lot he'll tell you, Sarge. I heard eighteen distinct bones bust when you biffed him that last one."

"Have to catch another," said Trace irritably. "Damn!"

"And here it comes, at the double," said Slough.

A light bobbed a block away. Bill gestured at the fallen helmet. "Look at that, a regular searchlight." The beam was reaching up to flicker on low-hanging clouds. Its source of power must be startlingly potent. Trace picked up the helmet and settled it on his own head, where it dropped and rested heavily on his ears. He stepped behind a maple tree between sidewalk and street. "Out of sight," he growled at the others.

THE second alien slowed, walked briskly, faltered, stopped. He called out a couple of questioning syllables in the avian-like tongue. Trace came out from behind the tree and shot the orange beam directly into the single great eye. In the second's grace he thus achieved, he stepped up to the creature and clipped it sharply, competently, on the button.

"That does it," he said with satisfaction. "We got it made."

He knelt, removed the helmet, and passed it to Slough. Then he took off the one that he himself wore and gave it to Bill. "Toss them someplace where the light won't show. Can't mess around trying to turn 'em off—and they might be a couple of booby-traps. Broadcasting stations with brims, that'd lead the enemy right to us." He heaved up at the greenie's middle. He whooshed with surprise. "Little help, Bill," he grunted. "This thing weighs about three hundred!"

With the magician's aid he stood up, holding the alien over one shoulder. He looked toward the far-off hill where the others were waiting; he was thinking of Jane Kelly. It doesn't matter a damn about the others, he thought, not even the girl Barbara; but that little teacher with the sensible shoes...

They went up to the theater and turned the corner and there ahead of them were many ducking, bobbing orange lights. A ragged line of aliens was approaching the town, had already cut them off from the hill. They ran, Trace heavily with the inert weight on his shoulder, and there were more coming at them from the other side, so that their only escape lay through an alley that ran beside the theater. Down this they pounded, Trace cursing the helmets that must have shot out warning signals when they were removed; the aliens were coming too fast and purposefully for it to be accidental.

The alley debouched into another, but this was spotted at the ends by more headlamps. Bill felt a cold touching him that was deeper and more icy than the January wind. He said, "The movie's the last bet," and jumping to the back exit of the place, he performed a swift sleight-of-hand that every magician knows of, and the lock swung open, the hasp flipping back from the staple. He pulled at the door. Slough crept into the blackness, and Trace, still carrying the unconscious greenie, followed. Bill closed the door behind him. It was possible that the extraterrestrial marauders did not know the principle of the padlock, of course; in which case they might not notice the unlocked door. But Bill rather doubted it. So did Trace.

CHAPTER SIX

TRACE carried the feebly stirring alien along the aisle of the deserted theater, the others following behind him. He went up the stairs to the balcony and found the entrance to the projection booth; negotiated those narrow steps and dumped his captive unceremoniously on the floor between the two big projectors.

"No lock," said Bill, examining the door.

"The place is a trap," said Trace irritably. "Damn it...but there wasn't anyplace else to go." He knelt and rolled the green man onto his back and slapped his face hard. The alien opened his great eye dazedly, stared round at the three earthlings, and croaked, "What occur?"

"English!" gasped Bill.

"Sure," said Trace. "I expected it. Their emissary learned it and must have broadcast it to 'em while he was being taught. The helmets, the helmets. It's logical."

"Chwefft is told English," said the green man, "we talk English all." He put a hand to his head, and his tight mouth was drawn open into an oval of surprise. "Hat?" he said uncertainly.

"The first one beamed it to the fleet," agreed Slough. "That makes our job easier."

"How?" asked Bill.

"Knowledge, boy, the acquiring of knowledge."

The green man made as if to get up. Trace shoved him back. The creature came away from the floor at him like an enraged panther, striking up with little skill but immense strength at his head and chest. Trace dodged through the perfunctory guard and belted him on the nose, then, as his struggles merely increased, let him have a left cross high on the cheek, just grazing the rim of the eye. The alien cringed and held up his hands in supplication.

"Lousy fighter," said Bill.

"If you think so. I'll time the two of you for a couple rounds," said Trace savagely. "He's scared of his eye being touched; it must be sensitive as hell. Besides, we've got two of those pistols of theirs now, and he's no fool."

"Allow go," said the man on the floor. "Not keep."

"First you talk," said Trace, trying to keep basic English. "How many of you are there?"

"How many? Ah," the thing said, giving a curious one-eyed frown. He had no hair on his head and only a bald ridge for an eyebrow. *"How many* indicating number?"

"That's right."

"Not knowing word for how many. More than you," he said, "more on voyage than you, and more more at home."

"Home? Where's home?"

"The system Lluagor, home planet Chwosst," said the other, sitting up cautiously and clasping his knees. He smiled. His expression said clearly, if these insignificant mites want to question me, what harm can it do? Trace, fighting a surge of Irish rage, went on. Bill prowled over to the openings that showed the deserted theater, squinting through the gloom. They had turned on the lights in the projection booth, and that worried him, for the searchers might come in below at any minute. He found the house lights and threw them on, so that the booth would not glow a warning. Thank heaven the power plant's still working, he thought. As Trace hammered at the green man with questions, Bill began tinkering with the machines.

BIRD-FOOT was saying, in his unpleasant tones, "How many saucers about twenty to forty thousand, this worked out by our mathematicians Chwefft and Hlamnig after learning your system of numbers. Interesting primitive system without knowing sub-space and lacking even name for *fpiolhesit.*"

"Sub-space!" exclaimed Slough, darting forward until he stood directly before the alien. "How did he learn the name for that concept, I wonder? But it makes sense. Certainly it would seem logical that such an advanced race would have conquered the mathematically conceived sub-space, in order to travel interdimensionally from galaxy to galaxy. How else could they go distances that even at light's speed would take a portion of eternity?"

The green man eyed Slough, his head cocked. "Intelligent," he croaked. "Come closer." He reached out a finger that was crooked as if to beckon, bumped it against Slough, and recoiled, an expression of dismay fleeting over his hard features. Then the olive-green skin smoothed out. "Ah. Small, small man. Not know."

"You got a looney," said Bill.

"He's not crazy," said Trace. "I had that sort of figured out before." He left the subject as Bill frowned at him, quite uncomprehending, and said to the alien, "What do you want here?"

"Your planet."

The words were rasped out without emotion, but they were as cold as the wind of January that played outside the theater. Trace said, "Why?"

"Need worlds, Chwosst long ago full, more worlds needing." He labored ahead, perfectly in command of the English he knew, seeking now and again for words beyond his ken, substituting others that were yet clear to the enthralled listeners. For five minutes he talked, and eight and ten, to the three humans in the projection booth; outside his bird-footed, one-eyed compatriots padded the empty town, whose inhabitants they had eliminated with the handguns that morning, down to the last dog and canary. Now they had found the dead alien and the two helmets, now they sought those who squatted in the theater; beyond the town lay the ravaged country, and across its face stretched the lines of thousands upon thousands of quiescent green saucers, some spied on by other survivors of humanity, others proud in a total destruction wrought by their all-shattering rays. Of all of this Trace Roscoe was aware, and still the story of the captive green man pinned him without movement to the closing trap of the theater. Once he thought of Jane Kelly. This thought he battled down, because Trace Roscoe was engaged in a war, and he couldn't have any personal dreams at all…

Gradually the queer speech of the world-assassin painted the portrait of his race, his mission, and his egocentric soul.

CHAPTER SEVEN

SO LONG ago that there were no words for the incredible period of time that lay between then and now, the planet Chwosst, fourteenth from the sun Tsloahn in the star system Lluagor, had become overcrowded to the point of danger. The dominant race of Chwosst was the two-toed one-eyed green men who called themselves Graken, which signified "The Mighty," or "All-Consuming." The other races of life on the planet were insignificant, small rodent-like beasts used for food by the Graken, which were wholly carnivorous.

They conquered the principles of space travel and sent out fleets of ships—these early craft were bullet-shaped, much as the designers of the first potential rockets of Earth had shaped their creations—and within a hundred-year space they had perfected these so that travel was negligibly dangerous. In their own system they had discovered one other planet capable of supporting their kind. This had given them a long breathing space, during which they hammered at the locked gates of the sub-space corridors. The Graken bred fast, though, too fast, and their two planets filled up before they had solved interdimensional travel.

There followed a long spell of civil war, revolutions that cut their numbers down fantastically and at last came near to exterminating the Graken entirely. While they were repopulating their double homelands, they made a peace among themselves that was never again broken. To assure it, they invented the headgear that broadcast their thoughts, and in a generation or two they had become a kind of ant horde, billions of individuals conditioned to a kind of community thought, a way of life in which every idea of every individual was passed on to those near him, shared and refined amongst so many thousands that a giant race-mind at last made its appearance, and no single Graken ever felt that *he* had conceived anything, but that *they* had done it.

This conjoint cerebration did not reach through space from planet to planet, and so the single-mindedness of the Graken was kept on its track by constant emissaries from one half of the race to the other.

Now a new terror arose for them: the rodents on which they had fed, a breed of beast even more amazingly fertile than the Graken themselves, were decimated by a plague; and nourishment became so scarce that extinction was threatened. Of course there were no rich or poor among the Graken, no money and no privilege, any more than there would be among a queenless ant tribe. So as one grew hungry, they all did. They might have fed half their people and let the other half starve, but that was not the Graken way. Now, at this most crucial time of their history, the secret of subspace was finally discovered, and the relatively simple manner of intra-time interstellar journeying was ascertained.

Patrols were sent out in the old style bullet-craft, but due to a lack of manual maneuverability in entering and leaving the galaxies now opened to them, the casualties were nine ships out of each ten sent out from Chwosst. Even so, another habitable planet was found within a matter of a few Earth months, and food (composed of the "inferior races" found thereon) brought back to the hungry system of Lluagor.

THE saucer-shaped spacecraft were developed and fleets, so numerous that each of the three worlds became hardly more than a vast landing-ground, were built. Two of every three able-bodied male Graken were trained as pilots, navigators, technicians and attack-masters. Patrols of from ten to fifty thousand ships left the base planets regularly, cutting through dimensions of sub-space in a search for new worlds that was, of necessity, haphazard; and yet which regularly discovered habitable globes in the limitless reaches of the universe.

No instruments had ever been developed by the Graken with which to ascertain the facts about a planet from a distance greater than a few thousand miles. Thus, to check on size, gravity, atmosphere, animal life and so forth, the patrols were forced to scan a world from just beyond its limit of attraction. One possible haven out of each hundred thousand planets checked was an excellent average, one in half a million more than usual. Some worlds accepted were smaller with less gravity, others had certain differences atmospherically; but the Graken were an adaptable breed, and readily conformed to such changes.

The one male Graken in three who was not taken for saucer duty became a shepherd, a breeder of food animals, or a scientist.

The females bred and raised their offspring and bred again; their fertile life extended over the years from fourteen to eighty-five, their gestation period was four months. The race was prolific... The need for worlds was continually urgent.

And Terra was an almost perfect duplication of the Graken's prototype home planet.

The last development in the Graken's marauding through the reaches of space was the actual kidnapping of the new worlds, the theft of entire planets and their transportation through sub-space into the star system Lluagor.

This had been conceived and perfected only a few generations before. The chain of Graken-inhabited planets had reached the sum of fifty-three, and travel between them had become tedious, arduous, and sometimes dangerous, for the ships used for ordinary traveling were fewer and of older patterns than the patrol vessels. The Graken found their communal minds drifting into widened channels, as direct contact became less and less. The pressing need was for a single system of worlds ranged about one star, in which travel would be easy and frequent. They therefore devised the kidnapping principle.

First, every planet unfit for Graken life in the system Lluagor was destroyed, leaving only two worlds spinning about the sun Tsloahn. Then, one by one, the new Graken planets were brought through subspace and dropped into the home system. This was done by a method that could not be made completely clear by the captive green man; the basic idea of which, however, was easy to comprehend.

A PATROL of no less than 20,000 saucers was brought within a mile of the world's surface. They hovered in open-filed lines, linked up until the planet was girdled by one continuous belt of ships. On a planet of the Earth's circumference, this would be about one saucer per mile. The ships were connected electronically in series, and at a button's push, a lever's throw, or a dial's setting in the control vessel, the saucers together with the captive world were shot through sub-space and into the system Lluagor, where they were fixed in an orbit around the parent star Tsloahn. The saucers then drew off, and the Graken owned another world, a new home for their waxing, fruitful hordes.

After two failures, in which planets already crawling with millions of Graken blew up while entering sub-space, the method of annexation was perfected and the remaining forty-nine planets were added to the first two, Chwosst and Csenfar, in the home system. Later acquisitions were brought to the base after any intelligent native races had been crippled or annihilated, and there, in the comfort and convenience of their own spaceways, the Graken mopped them up and settled on them, keeping alive any species that made acceptable food. The journey through sub-space and the orbit fixing did not affect the atmosphere or inhabitants of the planets in any way.

Up to this point, no humanoid (or even Grakenoid) races had been discovered during the many Graken space explorations. The possibility of humans being used or bred as Graken-food was left undiscussed. Cannibalism, even of this offbeat kind, might be repugnant to the green folk, even though race-murder of a second cousin breed like Man, was not.

The patrol fleets were not in touch with their home base, as communication through sub-space was impossible. This was established by repeated questioning of the alien prisoner, whose name was an approximation of the syllable Glodd.

Only chance had brought the patrol to the Solar system. It was so far from Lluagor—even by the dimension-cutting sub-space—that it might never have been found except for an accident in their navigation.

Terra had been conquered and ravaged and would now be kidnapped because of a slip of an alien finger on an unknown instrument panel!

CHAPTER EIGHT

"WELL," said Trace, sucking in his breath, "there is some hope."

"Where?" asked Bill Blacknight with deepest woe.

"Tell you later. Did I hear something out there?"

Bill jumped to the apertures and peered into the lighted theater. "There are half a dozen of 'em coming up the aisle," he said, "We are sunk."

"Not yet. What's that film on the reels there?

Bill gave him a glance that said he was out of his head; but he obediently walked over to the nearest projector, pulled the film reel out a little, and squinted sideways at it. "Looks like a feature. All ready to run." He then looked at the film can on the floor between the two projectors—two more reels were inside it. He bent over and examined them. "You want to entertain these lousy green hellions, Trace?" He shook his head. "My Lord, of all films to show 'em. *The Rise and Fall of the Third Reich*. I saw that eight years ago, and it stunk then—about three-fourths of it is old newsreel clips."

"I know. I saw it," said Trace impatiently. "I noticed the marquee outside and I've been thinking…can you work one of those gadgets? Those cameras?"

"The projector? Hell, yes. I used to work in the neighborhood theater back home. I can do anything in show business. You want sound too?" Bill, mystified, was trying to take orders without thinking about them.

"Yeah. Better start now. I want that ready to run as soon as we get a lot of greenies inside." As Bill began working over the projector, Trace scowled and did his best to remember the Grade B propaganda thriller that was mounted on the projectors. He'd been conned into seeing so long ago. If only he was right about the opening scene! Slough, at the view-holes, said, "They're crowding in. The lights must suggest our presence."

"Get the show on the road," snapped Trace. He stood up, but as he did so Glodd seized the opportunity, rose as though he was spring-propelled, and leaped for the stairs that led to freedom. Trace snatched at him, snarling; the Graken hit him with the flat of one big hand and Trace was hurled clear across the tiny room and into a stack of film cans. The one-eye slammed open the door and vanished down the steps, croaking like a buzzard in pain.

"Roll it!" yelled Trace at Bill. "Roll it! And throw up the sound as loud as you can, or we're stew for their supper tonight!"

The ten seconds were an eternity; then it was suddenly a chaos of noise in the theater, a crash of artificial thunder breaking out of nowhere to engulf the startled green men who choked the aisles and searched among the seats of main floor and balcony. Even in the projection booth, where the sound was muffled, the effect was that of some dreadful cataclysm. The thunder merged into a titanic roll of many military drums, and Trace barked, "House lights down!" but Bill Blacknight, the old showman, had already flicked them low.

On the screen appeared a countryside, through which a broad highway cut straight from the camera's position. Far down the road something moved, growing slowly and menacingly as the drums tattooed. The aliens were held petrified, staring with their great single eyes at the panoramic screen its black and white picture. Even Glodd had halted at the foot of the booth's steps, gazing immobile across the heads of his closest companions, all assaulted by the strange burst of sound.

TRACE stood in the open door, looking at their erstwhile prisoner. Glodd was their worst danger for the moment. There was no telling how much of their conversation about the movie he could have understood; yet even if he'd grasped none of it, he was still the only Graken who knew where they were—and he was not stupid. Trace had one of the ray pistols in his hand. Risking everything, he centered it on Glodd and hauled back the stiff trigger.

Glodd puffed into steam and fire without a sound.

Not one greenie turned his head to see. Not an eye flickered from the giant screen.

Trace prudently shut the door, and jumped for the nearest aperture to watch the movie unroll. Bill had managed to lift the volume of the film even higher, and like a hymn to pandemonium, a paean of ear-shattering volume, the drums roared from the screen. Now the movement on the two-dimensional roadway was closer, and the front ranks of countless marching soldiers could be seen. It was an old film clip taken in Germany many years earlier—Hitler's legions, goose-stepping grandly toward the camera in a world that was then at peace—however uneasily. The soldiers grew larger and larger as they neared. The drums remained like endless thunder, and with them there now lifted the hateful marching song of the Third Reich.

The green men broke. They fled to the lobby of the theater, croaking and squawking, and without doubt their thought-radiating helmets flung the fear and panic from one to another, filling the hall and passing through space and metal into the lines of saucers that lay across the continent and the world. At the theater entrance they were jammed into a struggling mass. One of the greenies used his pistol on the locks, and the wave of green erupted into the dark street.

There was no firing at the screen. The soldiers there had grown to quadruple human size. "Giants..." whispered Bill to himself. "They think they're giants!" Then aloud, over the racket from the screen, he said to Trace, "It's like those natives of India or wherever the hell it was, who ran out of the movie houses to get away from the locomotives that were ramming out at 'em from—"

"It's better than that," said Trace. Once more Bill felt that the sergeant wasn't telling something he knew; but again he shrugged and let it go. Trace was a smart boy and what happened from now on was up to him.

The Graken in the balcony had all tumbled and hurtled to the bottom; the last few stragglers were pounding across the small lobby, uttering their birdlike cries of fear. The German Army was enormous on the screen, now their boot-soles showed huge in the goosestep, now the song and the drums were almost unbearably stentorian. Trace Roscoe grinned widely as the first letters of the title and credits flashed out to an empty house. "Come on," he yelled, "hop to it, you two. I'd guess we have ten minutes to clear out of this town before the saucers rip it up. He laughed as they made for the steps. "First time the Nazis ever did anything good for anybody..."

CHAPTER NINE

THEY did get free of the town, but only just in time. The saucers came in very low, over the heads of the scurrying men, and the rays that lanced out of their bellies were phosphorescing yellow-green. They struck first at the theater, from which until that instant Trace could still hear the roaring of the sound track; then they began leveling the place from end to end, and if their weapons had been atomic, explosive, or any other known military projectile short of a javelin, then the fleeing humans would have died in their tracks. As it was, they were knocked off their feet time after time, were flung headlong to pick themselves up bruised and shaken. But close as the rays came, the men suffered neither concussion nor burns.

Sergeant Trace Roscoe admired the alien weaponry from his viewpoint as a professional soldier. They were the ultimate weapon if you wanted to destroy an objective without any profound after-effects, or if you had a pinpointed target you needed to destroy individually from its surroundings. The rays annihilated anything they touched, dissolving metal, pulverizing stone, boring even into the ground beneath, while leaving everything beyond the vaporized area inviolate. The Graken were some experts at the scientific business.

Some distance from the town they found it easier going, as the vibrations of the earth were less. They scrambled up the slope of the hill and stood together at its crest, watching the town disappear in green smoke and yellow flame. Then Trace heard—faint yet plain—a sharp report among the greater noises—a rifle shot! He oriented himself fast and ran in the cold darkness toward the place where he'd left Jane Kelly with four others and a rifle. For the first time the soldier in him was unimportant, the mission of revenge forgotten, while Trace Roscoe worried over a girl.

He needn't have fretted. She stood squarely on her excellent legs, cradling the heavy gun in two fine long hands, an expression of utter determination on her beautiful face; and opposite her in the murky night sat Johnson and Kinkaid and Barbara Skye, moving nothing but their mouths. Jane, oblivious to Trace's approach, was saying, "Wiggle a foot, anybody who wants it blown off…"

Trace quietly laid an arm over her shoulders, and despite her control she jumped.

"Good girl,' he said. "Damn fine girl." It was the only speech of affection he'd ever made, and it didn't sound quite as strong as he'd wanted, but she smiled up at him with relief and maybe a bit of affection in those dark eyes. "I lost Hafnagel," she said. "I'm sorry, Trace."

"It's okay. Did you kill him?" He saw nothing incongruous in that idea. She blinked and said, "No. I shot to stop him but he dodged out of sight."

"The saucers," whispered Johnson hoarsely. "They're attacking us."

"They don't know you're alive, Mac. They're smashing the Nazi Army," And he was damned if he'd explain *that* crack, he thought. "Now listen to me," he went on, talking in his sergeant's voice to these reluctant recruits. "We don't have much time left. We did something down there that may have convinced the Graken—the green ones— that there's a race of giants on Earth. They're blotting out a regiment of the giants, or so they think, but they are sure to believe there are more. So they'll probably want to kidnap this planet as soon as possible, so they can get reinforcements from their base for the big fight." Quickly and untechnically he told them how the Graken annexed worlds for their growing system in some far galaxy. "That may happen in the next ten minutes, or it may take a day or so for them to link up their chain of saucers. I'd say at a wild guess, we have an hour or so to disrupt up their plan. So we're going to attack the saucers—"

Kinkaid screeched indignantly. "What? When we could head for cover—live off farms—hide out in the hills—?"

"Get this through your miserable skull," bawled Trace. "If these bastards manage to get us into their home system, we will end up in one of two ways: we'll be hunted down and slaughtered like vermin, or we'll be caught and bred for food! There won't be any such thing as guerrilla warfare against them. They can let loose a billion or two of their people on every continent on the world." He stepped close to the cowering plump Kinkaid. "I tell you," he hissed angrily, "I think we have a chance to beat them even now. It has to be fast and it'll take every ounce of brains and every last muscle in this whole damn crew to do it. Now take hold of yourself, you lame excuse for a man, and remember that your breed—not your state or your country or your nationality, but your *species*—has been slaughtered by the millions; cut down, maybe half wiped out; and now it's heading for the finish, and we're probably the only ones alive who have any idea of the future at all! For God's sake, be a man. Come on and fight!"

KINKAID stared at him, his eyes round and frightened in the darkness. Then he drew a breath they could all hear plainly as it rasped in his throat. "All right," he said. "You tell me what to do and I'll do it."

Johnson nodded. "I'm sorry. I don't mean to be so...scared," he said to Trace. "I'll try to help too."

Well doggone, thought Trace with satisfaction. He figured they could be made into a fighting force, and so they had.

He briskly shared out the weapons: the revolver to Slough, the rifle with its three remaining cartridges to Johnson, a ray pistol to Bill and one to himself. Then without another word he led them down the hill toward the saucers, which were resting again in their long quiet line beyond the smoking ruin of the town.

Jane Kelly he kept close to him, helping her now and then down a bad stretch of rough, icy ground. Once she asked him, "Trace, why do you think they'll take Earth away so soon? Why have we so little time?"

"Logic. They haven't any reason to wait, and they may feel they have something to fear now. They'll want to wrap up their operations here soon. And—" He paused, and then with surprise he heard himself telling this woman something he had never said to anyone else: "I'm half Irish, half pure black Irish, and I haven't exactly the second sight, mind you, but I do get hunches and they do pan out. Sometimes I'm all crawling with hunches. Well, I am now. I get the feeling that time's closing down like a big steel bear-trap on us. My spine prickles and my flesh is inching around on my bones. It's awful danger we're in at this minute, Miss Kelly, worse than it's been till this minute. Who knows, maybe they're setting things into motion right now, and us fiddling around on a hillside!"

"Have you any "hunch" about whether we'll beat them?" she asked seriously

He growled something that sounded obscene. "No," he said, "I tell you true, I haven't the faintest notion regarding that. I only know we've been given a peep at their secrets, and if we don't foul the Graken, nobody ever will." Then he leaped down a steep place, and was silent.

CHAPTER TEN

AS THEY ran with loping strides across the frozen plain, Trace heard a shout behind him; he turned his head and there was Hafnagel, pounding after them and calling desperately. Trace slowed a little, jogged on until the big man had caught up with him. "I thought you lit out for the thickets," said Trace shortly.

Hafnagel panted. "I decided to throw in with you," he said. "I was lying out in the brush listening to you... I was scared and not thinking straight." He waved his hands, groping for an explanation for conduct he did not wholly understand. "You're crazy," he said, "but I have to go with you. A fellow's got to strike back, I guess. He can't take everything lying down."

"Come on," said Trace.

They neared the first saucer, which lay, a colossal green metal eye staring up at heavy clouds in the winter sky, quiet and yet aware. Bill Blacknight said, a crack in his voice, "Are they looking at us? Are they watching us, Trace?"

"Dunno. We're going inside. Remember, once a Graken sees us, the whole bloody tribe of 'em knows where we are. We've got to kill instantly, or knock the helmets off before we're spied, understand?"

"But a helmet sends radio message when it's removed," the midget Slough protested. "Those helmets called the aliens to them—"

"I doubt it," said Trace. "I think they're useless without a Graken head in 'em. Each of those beauties had a second or so in which to think *danger, danger!* Now let's find the way into this hulk." He turned away impatiently. There was no time to argue possibilities. There was only time to act, and maybe there wasn't even that.

Swiftly he completed a full turn around the silent spacecraft. He could see nothing that might be an entrance; the green metal, steel or whatever alloy might be tougher than steel, showed no crack or crevice. Lord, he thought prayerfully, we have to find it fast.

Slough said, "It must be one of the ports. Check the ports." He gestured to the rim of the saucer toward a thick border that widened every thirty feet to make an oval opening. These were perhaps two feet deep, and closed there by a smooth plate of metal, which Trace presumed would slide away in time of need to allow weapons to project or possibly to serve as rocket jet exhausts. The openings were large enough for man to pass through, even so large a man as a Graken. And if one of these was the spacecraft door, then it must be openable from the outside.

He set his group to checking each port; but Bill Blacknight stepped back a little, his mind buzzing. If I was a green one-eyed bird-foot, he thought, and I was trotting up to my personal saucer. I wouldn't want to peer closely at every damn port on the rim before I found the door, would I? Hell, I'd want some sign somewhere, a pointer I could spot without any trouble. Where would it be? Near the top, most likely, and it ought to be plain enough to see without squinting. He examined what he could see of the top of the ship. The center was a raised bump, round and wide. Bill felt his mouth twitch up with excitement as he saw that it was not a perfect circle; off to the left it pushed out into a sharp point, as though the circle were being pierced from within itself by an arrow. He ran to the section of the edge to which this indicator aimed, and found one of the ports directly in line with it. Softly he called Trace, who came at the double.

"This is it?" asked the sergeant. "Can't see any difference. How do you figure?" Bill told him, as he scanned the lip of the oval port for signs of a door. Nothing. "Boost me up," said Bill.

Hafnagel held him on his shoulders, and Bill leaned into the port and ran his educated fingers over the smooth surfaces therein. He found the lock, a raised set of thumbsized nodes and two bars that would not move for him. Frantically he searched his mind for every trick he knew of locks and bolts and all such mechanisms. He began trying various manipulations, all his years of magic concentrating in the flying fingers.

The metal plate slid without sound into the sidewall, leaving an opening through which a diffused green glow poured out into his face.

Bill thought of the peculiar way he had moved the node and bar, and node and bar... In all the world, it was not likely that any man except a trained magician would have touched them in the right sequence. He puckered his lips and whistled without noise.

Taking the initiative, Bill hoisted himself from Hafnagel's shoulders and wormed into the hole. The passage was slick without being actually greased, and within seconds he rose to his feet in the first room of the great disk.

Trace followed, then the others, Hafnagel coming last. They gathered in a taut, apprehensive group, staring about them.

The room was empty of life. There was no sound in the saucer save for their own quick breathing.

CHAPTER ELEVEN

WITHOUT a glance at the curious furnishings of the craft, Trace Roscoe headed for the door on the right-hand side. It was a tall rectangle, like an earth-made door, but without knob; as Trace came within a foot of it, it slid into the wall so briskly that he would not have touched it had he been coming at a dead run. Electric eye, or the same principle, he thought, striding forward.

Nor was there anyone in this room, which was plainly a sleeping chamber. Trace marched for the next barrier, but Slough darted over to investigate a narrower door, and thus discovered the first two Graken. The vanishing portal showed a lavatory, and the pair of greenies stared up, startled, from a massive washbowl, in which they had been bathing their faces and bare arms. Their helmets were slung on wall pegs. Both of them went for their pistols, but Trace, not so surprised as they, beat them to the draw. He fired over the tiny man's shoulder, and the Graken died, their flesh dissolving into steam and fragments.

Barbara Skye said her first word in an hour. It was triumphant, but quite vulgar. Jane Kelly said nothing, but she grinned at the other girl with appreciation.

Trace bethought himself of the old Western axiom, that one good man with a rifle was worth four good men with revolvers. He took the big sporting gun from Johnson, and, thrusting his ray pistol into the front of his shirt where it would be handy, walked purposefully at the next door. He had a feeling about this one.

He wasn't wrong. Three aliens grouped around a table, bending above some chart or mathematical calculation, turned, and rose as he stepped into the doorway. Two of them he blasted before they had glimpsed him, and the third he took in the face with a heavy slug just as the beast was opening his mouth to shout or challenge. The rifle echoed like artillery in the small room, and Trace thought with a momentary despair that it had likely been heard all through the ship. He stepped over the twitching corpses and went on.

This time the door opened before he had neared it, and a green man, ready and tensed, stood on the threshold with a gun in his big fist. Trace, caught for an instant unawares, went to his knees and jerked up his pistol; it shot its deadly thin stream of force on the heels of the alien's and he saw it strike the broad chest and begin to disintegrate the whole being. The Graken's shot had missed.

Well, it had missed *him*, Trace realized, as he heard the sharp gasps behind him. He looked and saw Kinkaid's headless body topple over between Barbara and Jane. It showed the incredible depth of the women's feeling for the fight that lay ahead, for neither of them screamed...

Shoulder to shoulder Trace and Bill Blacknight went through the room and their pistols' beams snaked out without sound together, as before them the control panels and intricate machinery of the pilot cubicle appeared behind three tall green-skinned Graken. Slough's revolver bellowed hoarsely behind them. Bill felt a tug at his coat, and later discovered that a great patch of cloth had been burned away by the enemy's rays. Johnson, half-crazed with anger now and gone quite berserk, plunged past them as they fired at the aliens and the last spitting stream from a pistol caught him in the belly and burst his body asunder.

They were in the control room, the six remaining Earthmen, and the door through which they had leaped would not close. Bill fumbled wildly at the jamb, at the edge that was flush with the wall, and then Slough said, "The bodies! Roll away the bodies!"

Hafnagel and Bill took the blasted corpses by the heels and dragged them out of the cubicle; then, having cleared the space near the door, it slid swiftly shut, leaving them outside. They went to it, it opened, and at last the six were together in a shut room.

Trace handed his pistol to Hafnagel. "Can you trigger it?" he asked, thinking of the man's stiff fingers. Hafnagel put out his hand and flexed it easily. "Don't ask me why," he said shortly. "It happened when we came into this thing." He took the weapon.

"Nervous release," said Trace. "I've seen it happen under fire." He turned to the bank of mechanisms, the sprawling panels full of controls. "Oh brother," he said under his breath. Then he went to work, trusting the others to guard his back.

Even when he heard Slough's revolver bang twice, he did not look up from the things he was working on.

CHAPTER TWELVE

THEY had killed nineteen Graken, and Slough, reloading the clumsy revolver with his tiny hands, presumed that the entire crew was not dead. They had killed nine on their way in here, and had finished off ten more since.

The queer part of it was that, although Trace had been sweating blood over the instruments for more than a quarter of an hour, no reinforcements had appeared from the other saucers. Slough did not understand this. Certainly a number of those perishing aliens had sent out frantic messages for aid before they died; and according to the late Glodd's story, such thought-calls should have been heard even over in Europe, Africa, or Asia, let alone in the saucers that were, so to speak, just next door.

The only answer seemed to be that one saucer was expendable. This, considering the Graken's mutual reliance, must mean that every other saucer was engaged in work of the utmost importance—such as forming the chain that would carry Terra through subspace into the system called Lluagor.

He handed his revolver to Jane Kelly. The girl was pale, but her features were set in strong, determined lines. Slough admired her; she was one of the finest specimens of womankind he had ever seen. "I don't think we can expect more visitors, my dear," he said to her, adding to himself, *unless we find ourselves in another galaxy.* "You keep this ready, however." He went to Trace Roscoe.

Trace said gruffly to him, "Don't need you. Get back there."

"Of course you need me. I was an airplane designer, remember? I have some knowledge. Have you found the electronic device yet?"

Trace turned up a lined and agonized face. After a moment he said, "No. Not yet."

"Keep going, then. I'll start at the other end," said Slough.

The banks and panels were far more intricate even than they had first supposed. Slough believed that the device they were searching for would probably be a type of klystron, considering the ultra-high-frequency application. Whatever turn the Graken's science had taken, he felt the principles of electronics, being universal, must be those involved in this sub-space travel; and it did not seem reasonable that an electronic mechanism would be very different on Chwosst or Terra or Mars or anywhere else.

Trace believed this too. He was a pretty fair student of electronics and he doubted that any race could disguise a high vacuum thermionic tube or an amplifying circuit or a thyratron in such a manner that he, Sergeant Trace Roscoe, couldn't identify it. The photoelectric cells that opened and closed the doors seemed to be of the same type as those used on Earth for the same function; Trace had taken two minutes to pry off the cover of the cell in the left wall and inspect the construction. So hopefully he would be able to discern what the "planetary kidnap-device" was when he came across it.

He glanced at his watch. More than half an hour had passed since they entered the ship.

Trace couldn't help feeling that the human race might be hanging on his fingers, which fumbled among a myriad of esoteric gadgets, in search of one that might be no more than a pair of resonant cavities, an anode, a cathode, and a grid. He felt his coolness departing, the sweat of latent terror stood on his face. He lost the tough-sergeant veneer and slowly became a panting, panicked man.

Then he caught the image of Jane Kelly out of the corner of his eye, and he bit his lip and told himself off in Gaelic cuss words He went back to his job again with a firmer grip—and in five minutes he found the device he was hunting.

"Slough!" he shouted, in the bull's roar that once had nearly drowned out the Red guns in Korea. "Slough, come here!" And the small man, who had been six steps away, bounded to his side with his blue eyes wide in astonishment. "Is this it?" asked Trace fiercely. "Am I right, is this it?"

Slough glared at the small recess, and softly said, "Aha…" It was an intricate and highly specialized form, if he was any judge, of the resonant cavity magnetrons with which he had worked often in the past. He nodded to Trace.

Trace nodded back and said, "Okay. Now we gimmick it."

"Can I help?" asked the midget, eager as a boy.

"You're damn right. My fingers are too big to get into all these crannies. Get in behind the tube, like so, with your index finger."

AS TRACE ordered and Slough obeyed, the others came round them, still alert for raiders, but eager to listen to the mysterious words that came, sharp and intense, from the sergeant's lips. Now and then Slough would disagree, and they'd argue; Bill began to fidget with apprehension. The scientific jargon was unknown to him.

"But if we lead in the wire from this other thing, which has got to be the fuel feed—"

"Why must it be? We don't know it is. I say build up the frequency of oscillation until—"

"Well, then, stick your damn fingers over here and hold this steady while I—"

And so on. Bill was certain that it would never end, that they must be caught at sunrise by an investigating party of the green aliens; but suddenly the midget and the soldier were moving off from the control banks, looking at each other with expressions half smug and half fearful. "Let's get out," said Trace abruptly.

"What did you do?" asked Jane Kelly, as they hurried through the rooms toward the entrance port.

"Gimmicked it," said Trace. His hand fell on her arm and squeezed reassuringly. "The electronic device is now altered so it'll build up an intolerable frequency; it's also connected with the thing we think is the fuel feeder, and with a row of buttons we're almost certain connect with the blasting rays."

They reached the port. "In other words," prompted Jane, "what?"

"In other words, when the ships are set to send Earth catapulting into the sub-space subways, this disk is going to blow sky-high; and since they're all connected in series electronically, the whole damn fleet should explode simultaneously."

They wriggled through the short passage, dropped to the ground. It was very dark on the plain. Patches of snow on the ground showed dark shapes of tree and bush and boulder; after the green light of the saucer, this outer world was dim and full of illusions. Jane thought she saw a Graken approaching, and stifled a scream when she realized it was the shadow of a swooping owl. She said loudly, "I don't like it."

"What?" asked Trace. They were standing in the shadow of the saucer, indecisive.

"I don't like this. It's too easy. It's a let-down." She grasped him by the arms, and he—startled—looked down into her face that was a lovely, softened blur in the night. "I'm half Irish too, Trace Roscoe, half pure black Irish; that's the Kelly in me. And I tell you plain, I feel wrong about this. It can't happen so pat, you can't just change a wire or two, hook up this and attach that, and foil the kidnapping of a whole world. There's something wrong, there's a thing missing that's vital."

"Baby," he said, so low that no one else heard, "I can tell you what it is. It's an interplanetary roulette wheel, with all our chips on one lone number.. Because there's about one chance in a thousand that what we did will actually work the way we want it to. That Graken machinery's out of this world. Half of what we did I can't explain even to myself. We just made a half-blind stab at wrecking their plans."

"It's something else. We're forgetting something." Her eyes suddenly went wide. "Oh, Trace," she cried suddenly, gripping him in anguish. "I know... I *know*.

"Well what is it, Jane?"

'It's that there's no replacement crew in this saucer. They never even came to fight us. That means they've either taken Earth into their galaxy already, or else that when the time comes, they'll do it without bothering about this saucer—and if that happens, where will our plan be?"

Trace almost sat down, his body went so limp. "Guess I never thought of that," he said resignedly.

"You've got to get a crew here," she said as the others crowded around. "You've got to get them out of their ships, no matter how busy they are, and let them see that they can take this ship back again. That they *should* take this ship back."

"She's right," exclaimed Bill. "We have to create a diversion to suck 'em out of their hidey-holes, Trace."

"The only way is to attack the saucers," he said wearily, "and how we do that with two ray guns and a revolver, heaven only knows."

"Why, we do it with two ray guns and a revolver, then," said Barbara suddenly. "Why not? That next saucer's maybe a hundred feet away. Take a shot at it, for Pete's sake. Try it and see."

Trace inflated his chest and once more he was the complete sergeant. He tore the pistol from Bill's hand, raised it and sent a streak of green death arrowing at the dark bulk of the nearby spacecraft. Playing it along the rim, he tried to strike the oval ports with it; and he did not release the trigger for a full minute. "Now let's see," he said. He looked at Jane and the redhead. "You two take off," he barked. "Head for the hill, pronto." His tone was so commanding that they immediately turned and ran, Jane twisting her head back at every third step. Shortly they were out of sight.

Nothing moved, and if there was any damage to the other saucer, it could not be seen from where the men stood. Trace, impatient, was lifting the weapon again, when a green light shone out from the center of the edge.

"Ah," breathed Trace. "We've raised 'em now let 'em come, don't stop 'em, and we'll man this death-trap yet!"

CHAPTER THIRTEEN

THEY lay in a kind of shallow ditch just under the outer edge of the great saucer; watching the orange lights from the helmets bob and duck nearer. Bill said quietly, "We're cut off from the hill now."

"That's okay. The women will wait; and we can fall back on the ruins of the town if they chase us. They may just investigate the ship here, and not bother with us. We are only vermin, after all."

Hafnagel said, "What if they see the changes you made in that panel?"

"They shouldn't, unless they look mighty close."

"And will it work?" asked the big man.

"Who the hell knows?" retorted Trace irritably. "Maybe it's too late now. Maybe we're spinning around Tsloahn already. Who can tell? We can't see the stars, the clouds are too thick."

The aliens were very close now and the four men fell silent. The lamps drew up to the deserted ship, hesitated, and at last one lifted and disappeared, as its wearer vanished into the open port. Trace shut his eyes and said a quick private prayer of thanksgiving; then he whispered, "We're okay now. Let's head for the ruins." They crawled out of the ditch and, their work done, made for the empty wreckage at top speed.

Behind them a shout went up, a raucous croak of triumph. Then a voice said weirdly in English, pitched high and carrying, "Not run, die!"

Trace got the idea, disagreed with it, and put all his strength into a terrific sprint. He found himself bathed in orange radiance, as the distant Graken focused their helmet beams. Just before the first green ray was fired, he saw a very low wall of bricks miraculously uncrumbled, made for it, hurled himself over, and landed on his chest with a scarce-felt smack of pain. The others followed him, and hugged dirt as the ray guns sliced the cold air harmlessly.

After a while the orange glow went away. Trace cautiously looked over the wall. He couldn't see anything—but he had a feeling. The pursuing aliens hadn't all retreated into their ships, he knew that.

He was not quite unprepared, therefore, when the Graken came over the bricks on top of him.

It was probably the largest and heaviest of all those whom Trace had seen. It fell on him like the side of a collapsing barn, and Trace felt all his breath leave his lungs in one excruciating wheeze. He fought to bring the muzzle of the ray gun against it, but could not move his arm, which was pinned under the creature's knee. Only the soldier's left arm was free. He flailed a blow that landed solidly, but the alien only squalled and chopped at his face with its clubbed pistol. Trace felt skin and flesh give way along his cheekbone, felt blood gush from the slice of the metal. He heaved up as heartily as he could, at the same time aiming another left jab for the brute's face.

His knuckles took it square in the eye. It shrieked, reeled back on its knees, and Trace fought tigerishly and was free. He delivered his finest right cross to the throat, and the Graken writhed on the frozen earth. Then Slough and Bill were there—the fight had taken only seconds— and the magician in a frenzy of rage booted the green head with the toe of his heavy shoe. That was that.

Slough's voice said softly, *"Monstrum horrendum, injorme, ingens, cui lurmen ademptium."* He rolled the alien's body over so the big head came up into the dusky light. The broad single eye gaped blankly. "Virgil said that about another Cyclops, luckily of a mythical breed. A horrible monster, misshapen, vast, whose only eye had been put out." He sighed. "Trace, the only real work we had here is done, for failure or success it's finished, and we can't do any more good here. Let's go back to the women. If so be it our plan succeeds, they'll need you to watch over them in the—ah, the post-war world, which may be a little wild for a time. And if we've lost our gamble, then you should be with your girl when the end comes. You can't do any good by fighting guerrilla-fashion down here."

"My girl?" asked Trace, who had not realized how obviously he had been moon-calfing at Jane Kelly.

Hafnagel laughed. It was a joyous sound, the expression of a troubled man who had found release. "Go on, Sarge," he said, "Go to the hill, all three of you. I'll cover your withdrawal from here," He hefted the ray gun he carried. "Don't argue with me," he said before Trace could speak. "You know a retreat needs a rear guard—and I mean to have another Graken scalp or two before I quit. Go on."

Trace argued in passionate whispers; but shortly found himself creeping on all fours across the razed town, without fully remembering how he had left the wall. There was no sound or sign of movement on all the wide plain; and as they came to the beginnings of the slope, he said, "I shouldn't have left him. He ought to have come with us."

Then they saw in the distance the streaks of green fire, and a pair of orange spotlights which almost immediately went out. The ray pistols kept darting their beams along the ground, and Trace said again, "I shouldn't have left Hafnagel."

"He never meant to follow us," said Slough.

"It was right to leave him," said Bill Blacknight quietly. "You gave him a few minutes of glory. That's not a bad deal, you know."

When they crested the hill, the green shafts had vanished, and the plain was dark under the heavy clouds that hid the sky.

CHAPTER FOURTEEN

THE five of them sat on the lip of the hill, hunched up against the cold, clasping their knees and occasionally rubbing hands or ankles for warmth. Trace had one arm around Jane Kelly, whose dark head lay against his chest. He was almost happy. He thought he had lost, lost his vengeance and his universe, and still he was all but contented, because he had this girl close to him.

The saucers rested without motion on the plain. The clouds had thinned, the moon's location could be told by its misted radiance, but no stars shone and the humans could not tell whether they were spinning around Sol or Tsloahn. After all, as Trace had said, the moon might have been kidnapped right along with Earth—or it might be a different moon, or one of the other stolen planets in the Graken's home system.

Barbara hated stillness. She asked Trace, "How come those greenies thought your damned old movie was real? Couldn't they tell it was only a picture—them and their high IQ's?"

"No," said Trace. He roused himself and looked over at her. Bill Blacknight was snuggled against her (oh, for warmth...sure, thought Trace cynically) and the magician was obviously on the verge of the same strange happiness that touched Trace himself. "No," he said again, "they couldn't tell it was a picture."

"Why not?"

"Because they only have one eye."

"I don't see what difference that makes."

He assumed the role of patient instructor, dredging in his memory for the right words. "You need two eyes functioning as one organ to have what they call binocular vision. The retina isn't adapted for three-dimensional perception, see?"

"No," said Barbara.

"Well, to perceive solid things for what they are, you have to have two retinal images, thrown on both eyes by the one object you get help from linear and aerial perspective—if you know the size of a thing you can judge how far away it is—but supposing you don't know its size, you're liable to misjudge its distance if you've only got one eye. One eye, two dimensions; two eyes, three dimensions."

"I get that," said Bill sleepily. "How'd you happen to think of it, Trace?"

"It was Slough here. Two times a greenie made a mistake as to how far away he was from Slough—once on the street, when it didn't grab for him when it could have, and again in the theater, when Glodd motioned for him to come closer, and hit him accidentally. Both of them thought Slough was average human size. Both were looking at him from a low viewpoint, the first on its knees and Glodd sitting on the floor. That's when it occurred to me that their eyesight must be two-dimensional. Of course it wouldn't bother them on their home planets, where everything was known by size and aerial perspective filled in their deficiencies. Probably their navigational instruments made up for their lack of depth perception in flight, too. But when I turned the Nazi Army onto them, they were baffled. They must have thought giants were coming up out of a hole under the theater—which is why they ran like hell and then blasted the town."

"Very clever," said Slough. Jane echoed this, and Trace said to her, quietly, "I'm not quite the uneducated slob you might think I am, lady."

"I don't think anything of the sort! You're—you're a man, a fine, tough, intelligent man." She was so sincere she sounded angry. Trace glowed softly with pride.

THERE was a very long silence then. Nobody moved from their chosen vantagepoint. The hidden moon went down. At last Trace cleared his throat self-consciously.

"I'd like to ask a question myself. Of you, Slough."

After a slight pause, Slough said, "What is it?"

"Well, you're a little too smart a geezer for reality, if you know what I mean. You figured those helmets for thought-radios, when it was a fantastic possibility that no normal man would have hit on so quick with so little to go on. Then you did things with the electronic device in that saucer that I couldn't have come up with in a coon's age."

"I'm an engineer," said the tiny man. He chuckled. "And I read a lot of science-fiction."

"Okay. Then there's this. Thirty-odd hours ago you had a badly broken left arm, which I set for you and put in a sling." Trace spoke slowly, almost with fear now that he voiced his suspicions, "Sometime during our first raid on the town, you discarded the sling; when we were in the saucer, you fought, and afterwards you worked on the instruments with both hands. It's impossible, but it must be true—your arm knit completely within a day." He turned and bending over Jane Kelly he stared wide-eyed at the dark figure of the little man.

"Slough," said Trace huskily, *"what are you?"*

Slough sighed. "Whatever I am, Trace Roscoe, I am not your enemy. No, nor ever shall be, yours or your people's. Look!" He cried out so suddenly that the four of them, shocked, stared out in the direction in which he gestured. "The saucers," he said, "they're rising!"

"The gimmicked one?" asked Bill, whose eyes were bleary with lack of sleep.

"Yes, all of 'em," said Trace. He jumped up, hauling Jane to her feet with him. "It's coming, they're hoping to do it," he said, and he clenched his teeth and took a firm grip on the girl, as though he wanted to hold her on the earth when it shot into the uncanny regions of sub-space. "Hold tight," he said, with no particular sense but a vast deal of emotion. "Hold tight, Jane." And Jane held him tightly.

The saucers rose higher, dwindling in size; they reached the low cloud layer and passed into it, becoming hazy and then invisible.

Twenty thousand spacecraft girdled the globe, linked electronically, readied for flight with their stolen planet to unknowable distances of deep space.

The men and women waited, their breath emerging in brief white frosty spurts in the cold air. And nothing happened.

After twenty minutes, Trace put a trembling hand to his forehead. "We lose," he said. He saw Slough begin to walk away from them, going back along the gradual slope among the bare trees, but he did not even call after him. It didn't matter a damn now, what or who the midget was.

"We lose," he said again, and hugged Jane fiercely.

And then the sky exploded.

CHAPTER FIFTEEN

TRACE flung himself on the ground, sheltering Jane; he felt rather than saw that Bill had done the same with Barbara. He gazed up, and saw the great rack of clouds torn and dispersed by the force of the blast. There was a chain of brilliant green-white balls of light, like so many bursting skyrockets, that stretched from horizon to black horizon across his world. He thought of the shards of metal, the evil whistling splinters and hunks of meteoring death that would rain out of the sky after such a multiple explosion, and he buried his face in Jane's soft hair, trying desperately to cover her whole body with his own. The noise above them was so mighty a roar that Trace was deafened, and his head hummed and rang intolerably.

In that moment, oddly, he thought again of Slough, and realized what he must be. The Irish intuition, second sight, or what-have-you it works in a cockeyed way, he said to himself, waiting for the shower of molten hail.

Slough was of the extraterrestrials, too!

Oh, not the Graken, the wicked green one-eyed bird-footed destroyers. But he was a saucerman, right enough. Lord knew how many of them had been living among us before the Graken attacked. No telling how many had died, how many still lived.

Trace remembered the saucer sightings that had perplexed the Air Force so many years before. The blue-lit disks that soared and dipped and shot away from pursuit, the disks that had been seen by reputable folk for—well, possibly for centuries. Funny he hadn't thought of it before, but all those well-vouched-for sightings could not have been Graken. The Graken shot into our system no longer ago than late December! And all the long while before we'd been under the surveillance of *blue-lit* saucers—not green, but blue at night and silvery in the sunlight!

He wriggled, his body awaiting the impact of the metallic missiles, his mind occupied with Slough.

And if there'd been saucers here for so long, and even saucer-people among us, what had happened to them when the Graken came? Any space battles between warring saucers would have been seen. Had they retreated to their own planet at sight of the Graken fleet, through space or interdimensional sub-space? Maybe. Or maybe they'd hidden in or on the Earth.

Why hadn't they fought? The Graken had no allies in the universe. The blue-disk cowards had run! Except old Slough, if he were one, he hadn't run. Why had the great ships left Terra? Not their fight? Or...

Or suppose they couldn't fight! Suppose they had no weapons in their craft, no rays nor bombs—Trace exclaimed wordlessly as this probable truth occurred to him. The blue disks were only observers, they weren't warcraft. Perhaps their people had no weapons at all. Perhaps they were a nation of peace, as the Graken were a nation of eternal war. And their long watch over the world had been either curiosity, or hopeful friendliness.

In which case, they'd likely be back. Trace hoped they would; he had liked Slough. Terra could use friends now.

He jerked his head up and stared at the sky. Even if the Graken ships had been three miles up, their remains should have showered down to earth by this time. He got to his feet with a grunt. The gimmicking of the controls in that saucer had been better than he'd known; the ring of saucers had not only exploded, they'd been atomized.

TRACE helped Jane to her feet, as Bill Blacknight did the same for Barbara. "Well," said Trace, "let's not sit on our cans out here all night. Let's get this show on the road. We have a hell of a lot to do."

"Such as what?" asked Bill.

"Mac," said Trace firmly, "this is still the Army of the United States, and we got a world to police up. There'll be more left than us four; there'll be millions of people, here and on the other continents too, who'll need all the help we can give 'em."

"We can help the world?" asked Barbara. "Us four?"

"We've done a lot already," said Jane dryly.

"There's more, we haven't begun yet. We have to find a radio, get in touch again," said Trace, his voice strong and happy. "There ought to be some planes left, in private airports and out in the country. We've got to scrape together what's left of civilization and patch it up and make it better than it ever was. You know anybody that could do the job better?"

"No…" Jane said, "…darling."

Trace blinked. He was not a demonstrative man, but he leaned over and kissed her on the nose with haste and embarrassment. "Come on," he said, gulping a little, "we've got work to do."

They started off along the crest of the hill, and then Bill grasped Trace's arm and said in a whisper, "Oh, oh Lord, we forgot."

"Forgot what?"

"We may be in the Graken's star system, what the hell was it, in Lluagor! They took such a long time—maybe they got us there before they blew up!"

The four people searched each other's faces silently, and even Trace was too appalled at the thought to verify it for a moment. Then Jane Kelly turned her face up to the sky, where the clouds had been rent and scattered by the blast.

After a long moment she put her hand in Trace's.

"I'm not much of an astronomer, Trace," she said, her voice calm and sweet and proud. "But even so, I can recognize the Big Dipper when I see it." She pressed his fingers affectionately. "And I do see it," she said.

THE END

If you've enjoyed this book, you will not want to miss these terrific titles…

ARMCHAIR SCI-FI & HORROR DOUBLE NOVELS, $12.95 each

ARMCHAIR SCIENCE FICTION CLASSICS, $12.95 each

ARMCHAIR SCI-FI & HORROR GEMS SERIES, $12.95 each

If you've enjoyed this book, you will not want to miss these terrific titles...

ARMCHAIR SCI-FI & HORROR DOUBLE NOVELS, $12.95 each

D-91   **THE TIME TRAP** by Henry Kuttner
           THE LUNAR LICHEN by Hal Clement

D-92   **SARGASSO OF LOST STARSHIPS** by Poul Anderson
           THE ICE QUEEN by Don Wilcox

D-93   **THE PRINCE OF SPACE** by Jack Williamson
           POWER by Harl Vincent

D-94   **PLANET OF NO RETURN** by Howard Browne
           THE ANNIHILATOR COMES by Ed Earl Repp

D-95   **THE SINISTER INVASION** by Edmond Hamilton
           OPERATION TERROR by Murray Leinster

D-96   **TRANSIENT** by Ward Moore
           THE WORLD-MOVER by George O. Smith

D-97   **FORTY DAYS HAS SEPTEMBER** by Milton Lesser
           THE DEVIL'S PLANET by David Wright O'Brien

D-98   **THE CYBERENE** by Rog Phillips
           BADGE OF INFAMY by Lester del Rey

D-99   **THE JUSTICE OF MARTIN BRAND** by Raymond A. Palmer
           BRING BACK MY BRAIN by Dwight V. Swain

D-100 **WIDE-OPEN PLANET** by L. Sprague de Camp
           AND THEN THE TOWN TOOK OFF by Richard Wilson

ARMCHAIR SCIENCE FICTION CLASSICS, $12.95 each

C-31   **THE GOLDEN GUARDSMEN**
           by S. J. Byrne

C-32   **ONE AGAINST THE MOON**
           by Donald A. Wollheim

C-33   **HIDDEN CITY**
           by Chester S. Geier

ARMCHAIR SCI-FI & HORROR GEMS SERIES, $12.95 each

G-9   **SCIENCE FICTION GEMS, Vol. Five**
           Clifford D. Simak and others

G-10   **HORROR GEMS, Vol. Five**
           E. Hoffman Price and others

If you've enjoyed this book, you will not want to miss these terrific titles...

ARMCHAIR MYSTERY & SCIENCE FICTION CLASSICS
$12.95 each

C-40   **MODEL FOR MURDER**
by Stephen Marlowe

C-41   **PRELUDE TO MURDER**
by Sterling Noel

C-42   **DEAD WEIGHT**
by Frank Kane

C-43   **A DAME CALLED MURDER**
by Milton Ozaki

C-44   **THE GREATEST ADVENTURE**
by John Taine

C-45   **THE EXILE OF TIME**
by Ray Cummings

C-46   **STORM OVER WARLOCK**
by Andre Norton

C-47   **MAN OF MANY MINDS**
by E. Everett Evans

C-48   **THE GODS OF MARS**
by Edgar Rice Burroughs

C-49   **BRIGANDS OF THE MOON**
by Ray Cummings

C-50   **SPACE HOUNDS OF IPC**
by E. E. "Doc" Smith

C-51   **THE LANI PEOPLE**
by J. F. Bone

C-52   **THE MOON POOL**
by A. Merritt

C-53   **IN THE DAYS OF THE COMET**
by H. G. Wells

C-54   **TRIPLANETARY**
E. E. Doc Smith

If you've enjoyed this book, you will not want to miss these terrific titles...

ARMCHAIR SCI-FI & HORROR DOUBLE NOVELS, $12.95 each

D-121 **THE GENIUS BEASTS** by Frederik Pohl
THIS WORLD IS TABOO by Murray Leinster

D-122 **THE COSMIC LOOTERS** by Edmond Hamilton
WANDL THE INVADER by Ray Cummings

D-123 **ROBOT MEN OF BUBBLE CITY** by Rog Phillips
DRAGON ARMY by William Morrison

D-124 **LAND BEYOND THE LENS** by S. J. Byrne
DIPLOMAT-AT-ARMS by Keith Laumer

D-125 **VOYAGE OF THE ASTEROID, THE** by Laurence Manning
REVOLT OF THE OUTWORLDS by Milton Lesser

D-126 **OUTLAW IN THE SKY** by Chester S. Geier
LEGACY FROM MARS by Raymond Z. Gallun

D-127 **THE GREAT FLYING SAUCER INVASION** by Geoff St. Reynard
THE BIG TIME by Fritz Leiber

D-128 **MIRAGE FOR PLANET X** by Stanley Mullen
POLICE YOUR PLANET by Lester del Rey

D-129 **THE BRAIN SINNERS** by Alan E. Nourse
DEATH FROM THE SKIES by A. Hyatt Verrill

D-139 **CRY CHAOS** by Dwight V. Swain
THE DOOR THROUGH SPACE By Marion Zimmer Bradley

ARMCHAIR SCIENCE FICTION CLASSICS, $12.95 each

C-55 **UNDER THE TRIPLE SUNS**
by Stanton A. Coblentz

C-56 **STONE FROM THE GREEN STAR**
by Jack Williamson

C-57 **ALIEN MINDS**
by E. Everett Evans

ARMCHAIR MASTERS OF SCIENCE FICTION SERIES, $16.95 each

G-13 **SCIENCE FICTION GEMS, Vol. Seven**
Jack Vance and others

G-14 **HORROR GEMS, Vol. Seven**
Robert Bloch and others

THE ONLY CERTAINTY
WAS CONSTANT CHANGE

Her name was Greta Forzane. She was a combination party girl and psychiatric aide who worked inside a midget cosmos outside the known universe. Her job was to entertain and help soldiers from the Change War, which was a war between two mysterious time-traveling powers: The Spiders (Greta's side) and The Snakes (the enemy). The soldiers fought this war, not so much with weapons, but by going back in time to change the past, or going ahead in time to change the future. In this bizarre conflict, history was changed dramatically. The Nazis had already won World War II and the Roman Empire had been dismantled practically before it got started! But even with all this there was still only one certainty—nothing in history was written in stone.

Join master science fiction author Fritz Leiber for what is considered by many to be his finest work, "The Big Time," a wildly entertaining novel that won the 1958 Hugo Award for the best novel of the year.

ABOUT FRITZ LEIBER:

Fritz Leiber was born in Chicago, Illinois on December 24th, 1910. His parents (Fritz, Sr. and Virginia) had a very strong theatrical background, being part of a long-touring Shakespearean troupe. As a teenager, Fritz, Jr. studied philosophy at the University of Chicago. He later toured as an actor with his parents' acting company, Fritz Leiber & Co.

Not bound by the pull of his parents' acting careers, Fritz eventually became a top-flight sci-fi and fantasy writer. Leiber wrote countless other novels and short stories, but his career suffered at times due to bouts with alcoholism, including a "lost" three-year period in the late '60s and early '70s.

Writing top-notch science fiction and fantasy was not, however, the only field Fritz Leiber excelled in; he became an expert fencer, a poet, an actor on stage and in movies, and a champion chess player. His greatest accomplishment in the world of chess was taking first place honors in the 1958 Santa Monica Open Chess Championship.

After a long, sometimes tumultuous, but often distinguished career, Fritz Leiber died on September 5th, 1992 at the age of 81.

THE BIG
TIME

By
FRITZ LEIBER

ARMCHAIR FICTION
PO Box 4369, Medford, Oregon 97504

*For more information about Armchair Books and products, visit our
website at…*

www.armchairfiction.com

Or email us at…

armchairfiction@yahoo.com

CHAPTER ONE
Enter Three Hussars

When shall we three meet again in thunder, lightning, or in rain?
When the hurlyburly's done. When the battle's lost and won.
—Macbeth

My name is Greta Forzane. Twenty-nine and a party girl would describe me. I was born in Chicago, of Scandinavian parents, but now I operate chiefly outside space and time— not in Heaven or Hell, if there are such places, but not in the cosmos or universe you know either.

I am not as romantically entrancing as the immortal film star who also bears my first name, but I have a rough-and-ready charm of my own. I need it, for my job is to nurse back to health and kid back to sanity Soldiers badly roughed up in the biggest war going. This war is the Change War, a war of time travelers—in fact, our private name for being in this war is being on the Big Time. Our Soldiers fight by going back to change the past, or even ahead to change the future, in ways to help our side win the final victory a billion or more years from now. A long killing business, believe me.

You don't know about the Change War, but it's influencing your lives all the time and maybe you've had hints of it without realizing.

Have you ever worried about your memory, because it doesn't seem to be bringing you exactly the same picture of the past from one day to the next? Have you ever been afraid that your personality was changing because of forces beyond your knowledge or control? Have you ever felt sure that sudden death was about to jump you from nowhere? Have you ever been scared of Ghosts—not the story-book kind, but the billions of beings who were once so real and strong it's hard to believe they'll just sleep harmlessly forever? Have you ever wondered about those things you may call devils or Demons—spirits able to range through all time and space, through the hot hearts of stars and the cold skeleton of space between the galaxies? Have you ever thought that the whole universe might be a crazy, mixed-up dream? If you have, you've had hints of the Change War.

How I got recruited into the Change War, how it's conducted, what the two sides are, why you don't consciously know about it, what I really think about it—you'll learn in due course.

The place outside the cosmos where I and my pals do our nursing job I simply call the Place. A lot of my nursing consists of amusing and humanizing Soldiers fresh back from raids into time. In fact, my formal title is Entertainer and I've got my silly side, as you'll find out.

My pals are two other gals and three guys from quite an assortment of times and places. We're a pretty good team, and with Sid bossing, we run a pretty good Recuperation Station, though we have our family troubles. But most of our troubles come slamming into the Place with the beat-up Soldiers, who've generally just been going through hell and want to raise some of their own. As a matter of fact, it was three newly arrived Soldiers who started this thing I'm going to tell you about, this thing that showed me so much about myself and everything.

When it started, I had been on the Big Time for a thousand sleeps and two thousand nightmares, and working in the Place for five hundred-one thousand. This two-nightmares routine every time you lay down your dizzy little head is rough, but you pretend to get used to it because being on the Big Time is supposed to be worth it.

The Place is midway in size and atmosphere between a large nightclub where the Entertainers sleep in and a small Zeppelin hangar decorated for a party, though a Zeppelin is one thing we haven't had yet. You go out of the Place, but not often if you have any sense and if you are an Entertainer like me, into the cold light of a morning filled with anything from the earlier dinosaurs to the later spacemen, who look strangely similar except for size.

Solely on doctor's orders, I have been on cosmic leave six times since coming to work at the Place, meaning I have had six brief vacations, if you care to call them that, for believe me they are busman's holidays, considering what goes on in the Place all the time. The last one I spent in Renaissance Rome, where I got a crush on Cesare Borgia, but I got over it. Vacations are for the birds, anyway, because they have to be fitted by the Spiders into serious operations of the Change War, and you can imagine how restful that makes them.

"See those Soldiers changing the past? You stick along with them. Don't go too far up front, though, but don't wander off either. Relax and enjoy yourself."

Ha! Now the kind of recuperation Soldiers get when they come to the Place is a horse of a far brighter color, simply dazzling by comparison. Entertainment is our business and we give them a bang-up time and send them staggering happily back into action, though once in a great while something may happen to throw a wee shadow on the party.

I am dead in some ways, but don't let that bother you—I am lively enough in others. If you met me in the cosmos, you would be more apt to yak with me or try to pick me up than to ask a cop to do same or a father to douse me with holy water, unless you are one of those hard-boiled reformer types. But you are not likely to meet me in the cosmos, because (bar Basin Street and the Prater) 15th Century Italy and Augustan Rome—until they spoiled it—are my favorite (Ha!) vacation spots and, as I have said, I stick as close to the Place as I can. It is really the nicest Place in the whole Change World. (Crisis! I even *think* of it capitalized!)

Anyhoo, when this thing started, I was twiddling my thumbs on the couch nearest the piano and thinking it was too late to do my fingernails and whoever came in probably wouldn't notice them anyway.

The Place was jumpy like it always is on an approach and the gray velvet of the Void around us was curdled with the uneasy lights you see when you close your eyes in the dark.

Sid was tuning the Maintainers for the pick-up and the right shoulder of his gold-worked gray doublet was streaked where he'd been wiping his face on it with quick ducks of his head.

Beauregard was leaning as close as he could over Sid's other shoulder, one white-trousered knee neatly indenting the rose plush of the control divan, and he wasn't missing a single flicker of Sid's old fingers on the dials; Beau's co-pilot besides piano player. Beau's face had that dead blank look it must have had when every double eagle he owned and more he didn't were riding on the next card to be turned in the gambling saloon on one of those wedding-cake Mississippi steamboats.

Doc was soused as usual, sitting at the bar with his top hat pushed back and his knitted shawl pulled around him, his wide eyes seeing whatever horrors a life in Nazi-occupied Czarist Russia can add to being a drunk Demon in the Change World.

Maud, who is the Old Girl, and Lili—the New Girl, of course—were telling the big beads of their identical pearl necklaces.

You might say that all us Entertainers were a bit edgy; being Demons doesn't automatically make us brave.

Then the red telltale on the Major Maintainer went out and the Door began to darken in the Void facing Sid and Beau, and I felt Change Winds blowing hard and my heart missed a couple of beats, and the next thing three Soldiers had stepped out of the cosmos and into the Place, their first three steps hitting the floor hard as they changed times and weights.

They were dressed as officers of hussars, as we'd been advised, and—praise the Bonny Dew!—I saw that the first of them was Erich, my own dear little commandant, the pride of the von Hohenwalds and the Terror of the Snakes. Behind him was some hard-faced Roman or other, and beside Erich and shouldering into him as they stamped forward was a new boy, blond, with a face like a Greek god who's just been touring a Christian hell.

They were uniformed exactly alike in black—shakos, fur-edged pelisses, boots, and so forth—with white skull emblems on the shakos. The only difference between them was that Erich had a Caller on his wrist and the New Boy had a black-gauntleted glove on his left hand and was clenching the mate in it, his right hand being bare like both of Erich's and the Roman's.

"You've made it, lads, hearts of gold," Sid boomed at them, and Beau twitched a smile and murmured something courtly and Maud began to chant, "Shut the Door!" and the New Girl copied her and I joined in because the Change Winds do blow like crazy when the Door is open, even though it can't ever be shut tight enough to keep them from leaking through.

"Shut it before it blows wrinkles in our faces," Maud called in her gamin voice to break the ice, looking like a skinny teenager in the tight, knee-length frock she'd copied from the New Girl.

But the three Soldiers weren't paying attention. The Roman—I remembered his name was Mark—was blundering forward stiffly as if there were something wrong with his eyes, while Erich and the New Boy were yelling at each other about a kid and Einstein and a summer palace and a bloody glove and the Snakes having booby-trapped Saint Petersburg. Erich had that taut sadistic smile he gets when he wants to hit me.

The New Boy was in a tearing rage. "Why'd you pull us out so bloody fast? We fair chewed the Nevsky Prospekt to pieces galloping away."

"Didn't you feel their stun guns, *Dummkopf*, when they sprung the trap—too soon, *Gott sei Dank*?" Erich demanded.

"I did," the New Boy told him. "Not enough to numb a cat. Why didn't you show us action?"

"Shut up. I'm your leader. I'll show you action enough."

"You won't. You're a filthy Nazi coward."

"*Weibischer Engländer!*"

"Bloody Hun!"

"*Schlange!*"

The blond lad knew enough German to understand that last crack. He threw back his sable-edged pelisse to clear his sword arm and he swung away from Erich, which bumped him into Beau. At the first sign of the quarrel, Beau had raised himself from the divan as quickly and silently as a—no, I won't use that word—and slithered over to them.

"Sirs, you forget yourselves," he said sharply, off balance, supporting himself on the New Boy's upraised arm. "This is Sidney Lessingham's Place of Entertainment and Recuperation. There are ladies—"

With a contemptuous snarl, the New Boy shoved him off and snatched with his bare hand for his saber. Beau reeled against the divan, it caught him in the shins and he fell toward the Maintainers. Sid whisked them out of the way as if they were a couple of beach radios—simply nothing in the Place is nailed down—and had them back on the coffee table before Beau hit the floor. Meanwhile, Erich had his saber out and had parried the New Boy's first wild slash and lunged in return, and I heard the scream of steel and the rutch of his boot on the diamond-studded pavement.

Beau rolled over and came up pulling from the ruffles of his shirt bosom a derringer I knew was some other weapon in disguise—a stun gun or even an Atropos. Besides scaring me damp for Erich and everybody, that brought me up short: us Entertainers' nerves must be getting as naked as the Soldiers', probably starting when the Spiders canceled all cosmic leaves twenty sleeps back.

Sid shot Beau his look of command, rapped out, "I'll handle this, you whoreson firebrand," and turned to the Minor Maintainer. I noticed that the telltale on the Major was glowing a reassuring red again, and I found a moment to thank Mamma Devi that the Door was shut.

Maud was jumping up and down, cheering I don't know which—nor did she, I bet—and the New Girl was white and I saw that the sabers were working more businesslike. Erich's flicked, flicked, flicked again and came away from the blond lad's cheek spilling a couple of red drops. The blond lad lunged fiercely, Erich jumped back, and the next moment they were both floating helplessly in the air, twisting like they had cramps.

I realized quick enough that Sid had shut off gravity in the Door and Stores sectors of the Place, leaving the rest of us firm on our feet in the Refresher and Surgery sectors. The Place has sectional gravity to suit our Extraterrestrial buddies—those crazy ETs sometimes come whooping in for recuperation in very mixed batches.

From his central position, Sid called out, kindly enough but taking no nonsense, "All right, lads, you've had your fun. Now sheathe those swords."

For a second or so, the two black hussars drifted and contorted. Erich laughed harshly and neatly obeyed—the commandant is used to free fall. The blond lad stopped writhing, hesitated while he glared upside down at Erich and managed to get his saber into its scabbard, although he turned a slow somersault doing it. Then Sid switched on their gravity, slow enough so they wouldn't get sprained landing.

Erich laughed, lightly this time, and stepped out briskly toward us. He stopped to clap the New Boy firmly on the shoulder and look him in the face.

"So, now you get a good scar," he said.

The other didn't pull away, but he didn't look up and Erich came on. Sid was hurrying toward the New Boy, and as he passed Erich, he wagged a finger at him and gayly said, "You rogue." Next thing I was giving Erich my "Man, you're home" hug and he was kissing me and cracking my ribs and saying, "*Liebchen! Doppchen!*" which was fine with me because I do love him and I'm a good lover and as much a Doubleganger as he is.

We had just pulled back from each other to get a breath—his blue eyes looked so sweet in his worn face—when there was a thud behind us. With the snapping of the tension, Doc had fallen off his bar stool and his top hat was over his eyes. As we turned to chuckle at him, Maud squeaked and we saw that the Roman had walked straight up against the Void and was marching along there steadily without gaining a foot, like it does happen, his black uniform melting into that inside-your-head gray.

Maud and Beau rushed over to fish him back, which can be tricky. The thin gambler was all courtly efficiency again. Sid supervised from a distance.

"What's wrong with him?" I asked Erich.

He shrugged. "Overdue for Change Shock. And he was nearest the stun guns. His horse almost threw him. *Mein Gott*, you should have seen Saint Petersburg, *Liebchen*: the Nevsky Prospekt, the canals flying by like reception carpets of blue sky, a cavalry troop in blue and gold that blundered across our escape, fine women in furs and ostrich plumes, a monk with a big tripod and his head under a hood—it gave me the horrors seeing all those Zombies flashing past and staring at me in that sick unawakened way they have, and knowing that some of them, say the photographer, might be Snakes."

Our side in the Change War is the Spiders, the other side is the Snakes, though all of us—Spiders and Snakes alike—are Doublegangers and Demons too, because we're cut out of our lifelines in the cosmos. Your lifeline is all of you from birth to death. We're Doublegangers because we can operate both in the cosmos and outside of it, and Demons because we act reasonably alive while doing so—which the Ghosts don't. Entertainers and Soldiers are all Demon-Doublegangers, whichever side they're on—though they say the Snake Places are simply ghastly. Zombies are dead people whose lifelines lie in the so-called past.

"What were you doing in Saint Petersburg before the ambush?" I asked Erich. "That is, if you can talk about it."

"Why not? We were kidnapping the infant Einstein back from the Snakes in 1883. Yes, the Snakes got him, *Liebchen*, only a few sleeps back, endangering the West's whole victory over Russia—"

"—which gave your dear little Hitler the world on a platter for fifty years and got me loved to death by your sterling troops in the Liberation of Chicago—"

"—but which leads to the ultimate victory of the Spiders and the West over the Snakes and Communism, *Liebchen*, remember that. Anyway, our counter-snatch didn't work. The Snakes had guards posted—most unusual and we weren't warned. The whole thing was a great mess. No wonder Bruce lost his head—not that it excuses him."

"The New Boy?" I asked. Sid hadn't got to him and he was still standing with hooded eyes where Erich had left him, a dark pillar of shame and rage.

"*Ja*, a lieutenant from World War One. An Englishman."

"I gathered that," I told Erich. "Is he really effeminate?"

"*Weibischer?*" He smiled. "I had to call him something when he said I was a coward. He'll make a fine Soldier—only needs a little more shaping."

"You men are so original when you spat." I lowered my voice. "But you shouldn't have gone on and called him a Snake, Erich mine."

"*Schlange?*" The smile got crooked. "Who knows—about any of us? As Saint Petersburg showed me, the Snakes' spies are getting cleverer than ours." The blue eyes didn't look sweet now. "Are you, *Liebchen*, really nothing more than a good loyal Spider?"

"Erich!"

"All right, I went too far—with Bruce and with you too. We're all hacked these days, riding with one leg over the breaking edge."

Maud and Beau were supporting the Roman to a couch, Maud taking most of his weight, with Sid still supervising and the New Boy still sulking by himself. The New Girl should have been with him, of course, but I couldn't see her anywhere and I decided she was probably having a nervous breakdown in the Refresher, the little jerk.

"The Roman looks pretty bad, Erich," I said.

"Ah, Mark's tough. Got virtue, as his people say. And our little starship girl will bring him back to life if anybody can and if..."

"...you call this living," I filled in dutifully.

He was right. Maud had fifty-odd years of psychomedical experience, 23rd Century at that. It should have been Doc's job, but that was fifty drunks back.

"Maud and Mark, that will be an interesting experiment," Erich said. "Reminiscent of Goering's with the frozen men and the naked gypsy girls."

"You are a filthy Nazi. She'll be using electrophoresis and deep suggestion, if I know anything."

"How will you be able to know anything, *Liebchen*, if she switches on the couch curtains, as I perceive she is preparing to do?"

"Filthy Nazi I said and meant."

"Precisely." He clicked his heels and bowed a millimeter. "Erich Friederich von Hohenwald, *Oberleutnant* in the army of the Third Reich. Fell at Narvik, where he was Recruited by the Spiders. Lifeline lengthened by a Big Change after his first death and at latest report Commandant of Toronto, where he maintains extensive baby farms to provide him with breakfast meat, if you believe the handbills of the *voyageurs* underground. At your service."

"Oh, Erich, it's all so lousy," I said, touching his hand, reminded that he was one of the unfortunates Resurrected from a point in their lifelines well before their deaths—in his case, because the date of his death had been shifted forward by a Big Change after his Resurrection. And as every Demon finds out, if he can't imagine it beforehand, it is pure hell to remember your future, and the shorter the time between your Resurrection and your death back in the cosmos, the better. Mine, bless Bab-ed-Din, was only an action-packed ten minutes on North Clark Street.

Erich put his other hand lightly over mine. "Fortunes of the Change War, *Liebchen*. At least I'm a Soldier and sometimes assigned to future operations—though why we should have this monomania about our future personalities back there, I don't know. Mine is a stupid *Oberst*, thin as paper—and frightfully indignant at the *voyageurs*! But it helps me a little if I see him in perspective and at least I get back to the cosmos pretty regularly, *Gott sei Dank*, so I'm better off than you Entertainers."

I didn't say aloud that a Changing cosmos is worse than none, but I found myself sending a prayer to the Bonny Dew for my father's repose, that the Change Winds would blow lightly across the lifeline of Anton A. Forzane, professor of physiology, born in Norway and buried in Chicago. Woodlawn Cemetery is a nice gray spot.

"That's all right, Erich," I said. "We Entertainers Got Mittens too."

He scowled around at me suspiciously, as if he were wondering whether I had all my buttons on.

"Mittens?" he said. "What do you mean? I'm not wearing any. Are you trying to say something about Bruce's gloves—which incidentally seem to annoy him for some reason. No, seriously, Greta, why do you Entertainers need mittens?"

"Because we get cold feet sometimes. At least I do. Got Mittens, as I say."

A sickly light dawned in his Prussian puss. He muttered, "Got mittens... *Gott mit uns*... God with us," and roared softly, "Greta, I don't know how I put up with you, the way you murder a great language for cheap laughs."

"You've got to take me as I am," I told him. "mittens and all, thank the Bonny Dew..." And hastily explained, "...that's French—*le bon Dieu*—the good God—don't hit me. I'm not going to tell you any more of my secrets."

He laughed feebly, like he was dying.

"Cheer up," I said. "I won't be here forever, and there are worse places than the Place."

He nodded grudgingly, looking around. "You know what, Greta, if you'll promise not to make some dreadful joke out of it: on operations, I pretend I'll soon be going backstage to court the world-famous ballerina Greta Forzane."

He was right about the backstage part. The Place is a regular theater-in-the-round with the Void for an audience, the Void's gray hardly disturbed by the screens masking Surgery (Ugh!), Refresher and Stores. Between the last two are the bar and kitchen and Beau's piano. Between Surgery and the sector where the Door usually appears are the shelves and taborets of the Art Gallery. The control divan is stage center. Spaced around at a fair distance are six big low couches—one with its curtains now shooting up into the gray—and a few small tables. It is like a ballet set and the crazy costumes and characters that turn up don't ruin the illusion. By no means. Diaghilev would have hired most of them for the Ballet Russe on first sight, without even asking them whether they could keep time to music.

CHAPTER TWO
A Right-hand Glove

Last week in Babylon, Last night in Rome,
—Hodgson

Beau had gone behind the bar and was talking quietly at Doc, but with his eyes elsewhere, looking very sallow and professional in his white, and I thought—Damballa!—I'm in the French Quarter. I couldn't see the New Girl. Sid was at last getting to the New Boy after the fuss about Mark. He threw me a sign and I started over with Erich in tow.

"Welcome, sweet lad. Sidney Lessingham's your host, and a fellow Englishman. Born in King's Lynn, 1564, schooled at Cambridge, but London was the life and death of me, though I outlasted Bessie, Jimmie, Charlie, and Ollie almost. And what a life! By turns a clerk, a spy, a bawd—the two trades are hand in glove—a poet of no account, a beggar, and a peddler of resurrection tracts. Beau Lassiter, our throats are tinder!"

At the word "poet," the New Boy looked up, but resentfully, as if he had been tricked into it.

"And to spare your throat for drinking, sweet gallant, I'll be so bold as to guess and answer one of your questions," Sid rattled on. "Yes, I knew Will Shakespeare—we were of an age—and he was such a modest, mind-your-business rogue that we all wondered whether he really did write those plays. Your pardon, 'faith, but that scratch might be looked to."

Then I saw that the New Girl hadn't lost her head, but gone to Surgery (Ugh!) for a first-aid tray. She reached a swab toward the New Boy's sticky cheek, saying rather shrilly, "If I might…"

Her timing was bad. Sid's last words and Erich's approach had darkened the look in the young Soldier's face and he angrily swept her arm aside without even glancing at her. Erich squeezed my arm. The tray clattered to the floor—and one of the drinks that Beau was bringing almost followed it. Ever since the New Girl's arrival, Beau had been figuring that she was his responsibility, though I don't think the two of them had reached an agreement yet. Beau was especially set on it because I was thick with Sid at the time and Maud with Doc, she loving tough cases.

"Easy now, lad, and you love me!" Sid thundered, again shooting Beau the "Hold it" look. "She's just a poor pagan trying to comfort you. Swallow your bile, you black villain, and perchance it will turn to poetry. Ah, did I touch you there? Confess, you are a poet."

There isn't much gets by Sid, though for a second I forgot my psychology and wondered if he knew what he was doing with his insights.

"Yes, I'm a poet, all right," the New Boy roared. "I'm Bruce Marchant, you bloody Zombies. I'm a poet in a world where even the lines of the King James and your precious Will whom you use for laughs aren't safe from Snakes' slime and the Spiders' dirty legs. Changing our history, stealing our certainties, claiming to be so blasted all-knowing and best intentioned and efficient, and what does it lead to? This bloody SI glove!"

He held up his black-gloved left hand which still held the mate and he shook it.

"What's wrong with the Spider Issue gauntlet, heart of gold?" Sid demanded. "And you love us, tell us." While Erich laughed, "Consider yourself lucky, *Kamerad*. Mark and I didn't draw any gloves at all."

"What's wrong with it?" Bruce yelled. "The bloody things are both lefts!" He slammed it down on the floor.

We all howled, we couldn't help it. He turned his back on us and stamped off, though I guessed he would keep out of the Void. Erich squeezed my arm and said between gasps, "*Mein Gott, Liebchen*, what have I always told you about Soldiers? The bigger the gripe, the smaller the cause! It is infallible!"

One of us didn't laugh. Ever since the New Girl heard the name Bruce Marchant, she'd had a look in her eyes like she'd been given the sacrament. I was glad she'd got interested in something, because she'd been pretty much of a snoot and a wet blanket up until now, although she'd come to the Place with the recommendation of having been a real whoopee girl in London and New York in the Twenties. She looked disapprovingly at us as she gathered up the tray and stuff, not forgetting the glove, which she placed on the center of the tray like a holy relic.

Beau cut over and tried to talk to her, but she ghosted past him and once again he couldn't do anything because of the tray in his hands. He came over and got rid of the drinks quick. I took a big gulp right away because I saw the New Girl stepping through the screen into Surgery and I hate to be reminded we have it and I'm glad Doc is too drunk to use it, some of the Arachnoid surgical techniques being very sickening as I know only too well from a personal experience that is number one on my list of things to be forgotten.

By that time, Bruce had come back to us, saying in a carefully hard voice, "Look here, it's not the dashed glove itself, as you very well know, you howling Demons."

"What is it then, noble heart?" Sid asked, his grizzled gold beard heightening the effect of innocent receptivity.

"It's the principle of the thing," Bruce said, looking around sharply, but none of us cracked a smile. "It's this mucking inefficiency and death of the cosmos—and don't tell me that isn't in the cards!—masquerading as benign omniscient authority. The Spiders—and we don't know who they are ultimately; it's just a name; we see only agents like ourselves—the Spiders pluck us from the quiet graves of our lifelines—"

"Is that bad, lad?" Sid murmured, innocently straight-faced.

"—and Resurrect us if they can and then tell us we must fight another time-traveling power called the Snakes—just a name, too—which is bent on perverting and enslaving the whole cosmos, past, present and future."

"And isn't it, lad?"

"Before we're properly awake, we're Recruited into the Big Time and hustled into tunnels and burrows outside our space-time, these miserable closets, gray sacks, puss pockets—no offense to this Place—that the Spiders have created, maybe by gigantic implosions, but no one knows for certain, and then we're sent off on all sorts of missions into the past and future to change history in ways that are supposed to thwart the Snakes."

"True, lad."

"And from then on, the pace is so flaming hot and heavy, the shocks come so fast, our emotions are wrenched in so many directions, our public and private metaphysics distorted so insanely, the deepest thread of reality we cling to tied in such bloody knots, that we never can get things straight."

"We've all felt that way, lad," Sid said soberly; Beau nodded his sleek death's head; "You should have seen me, *Kamerad*, my first fifty sleeps," Erich put in; while I added, "Us girls, too, Bruce."

"Oh, I know I'll get hardened to it, and don't think I can't. It's not that," Bruce said harshly. "And I wouldn't mind the personal confusion, the mess it's made of my spirit, I wouldn't even mind remaking history and destroying priceless, once-called imperishable beauties of the past, if I felt it were for the best. The Spiders assure us that, to thwart the Snakes, it is all-important that the West ultimately defeat the East. But what have they done to achieve this? I'll give you some beautiful examples. To stabilize power in the early Mediterranean world, they have built up Crete at the expense of Greece, making Athens a ghost city, Plato a trivial fabulist, and putting all Greek culture in a minor key."

"You got time for culture?" I heard myself say and I clapped my hand over my mouth in gentle reproof.

"But *you* remember the dialogues, lad," Sid observed. "And rail not at Crete—I have a sweet Keftian friend."

"For how long will I remember Plato's dialogues? And who after me?" Bruce challenged. "Here's another. The Spiders want Rome powerful and, to date, they've helped Rome so much that she collapses in a blaze of German and Parthian invasions a few years after the death of Julius Caesar."

This time it was Beau who butted in. Most everybody in the Place loves these bull sessions. "You omit to mention, sir, that Rome's newest downfall is directly due to the Unholy Triple Alliance the Snakes have fomented between the Eastern Classical World, Mohammedanized Christianity, and Marxist Communism, trying to pass the torch of power futurewards by way of Byzantium and the Eastern Church, without ever letting it pass into the hands of the Spider West. That, sir, is the Snakes' Three-Thousand-Year Plan which we are fighting against, striving to revive Rome's glories."

"Striving is the word for it," Bruce snapped. "Here's yet another example. To beat Russia, the Spiders kept England and America out of World War Two, thereby ensuring a German invasion of the New World and creating a Nazi empire stretching from the salt mines of Siberia to the plantations of Iowa, from Nizhni Novgorod to Kansas City!"

He stopped and my short hairs prickled. Behind me, someone was chanting in a weird spiritless voice, like footsteps in hard snow.

"*Salz, Salz, bringe Salz. Kein' Peitsch', gnädige Herren. Salz, Salz, Salz.*"

I turned and there was Doc waltzing toward us with little tiny steps, bent over so low that the ends of his shawl touched the floor, his head crooked up sideways and looking through us.

I knew then, but Erich translated softly. "'Salt, salt, I bring salt. No whip, merciful sirs.' He is speaking to my countrymen in their language." Doc had spent his last months in a Nazi-operated salt mine.

He saw us and got up, straightening his top hat very carefully. He frowned hard while my heart thumped half a dozen times. Then his face slackened, he shrugged his shoulders and muttered, "*Nichevo.*"

"And it does not matter, sir," Beau translated, but directing his remark at Bruce. "True, great civilizations have been dwarfed or broken by the Change War. But others, once crushed in the bud, have bloomed. In the 1870s, I traveled a Mississippi that had never known Grant's gunboats. I studied piano, languages, and the laws of chance under the greatest European masters at the University of Vicksburg."

"And you think your pipsqueak steamboat culture is compensation for—" Bruce began but, "Prithee none of that, lad," Sid interrupted smartly. "Nations are as equal as so many madmen or drunkards, and I'll drink dead drunk the man who disputes me. Hear reason: nations are not so puny as to shrivel and vanish at the first tampering with their past, no, nor with the tenth. Nations are monsters, boy, with guts of iron and nerves of brass. Waste not your pity on them."

"True indeed, sir," Beau pressed, cooler and keener for the attack on his Greater South. "Most of us enter the Change World with the false metaphysic that the slightest change in the past—a grain of dust misplaced—will transform the whole future. It is a long while before we accept with our minds as well as our intellects the law of the Conservation of Reality: that when the past is changed, the future changes barely enough to adjust, barely enough to admit the new data. The Change Winds meet maximum resistance always. Otherwise the first operation in Babylonia would have wiped out New Orleans, Sheffield, Stuttgart, and Maud Davies' birthplace on Ganymede!

"Note how the gap left by Rome's collapse was filled by the imperialistic and Christianized Germans. Only an expert Demon historian can tell the difference in most ages between the former Latin and the present Gothic Catholic Church. As you yourself, sir, said of Greece, it is as if an old melody were shifted into a slightly different key. In the wake of a Big Change, cultures and individuals are transposed, it's true, yet in the main they continue much as they were, except for the usual scattering of unfortunate but statistically meaningless accidents."

"All right, you bloody savants—maybe I pushed my point too far," Bruce growled. "But if you want variety, give a thought to the rotten methods we use in our wonderful

Change War. Poisoning Churchill and Cleopatra. Kidnapping Einstein when he's a baby."

"The Snakes did it first," I reminded him.

"Yes, and we copied them. How resourceful does that make us?" he retorted, arguing like a woman. "If we need Einstein, why don't we Resurrect him, deal with him as a man?"

Beau said, serving his culture in slightly thicker slices, "*Pardonnez-moi*, but when you have enjoyed your status as Doubleganger a *soupçon* longer, you will understand that great men can rarely be Resurrected. Their beings are too crystallized, sir, their lifelines too tough."

"Pardon me, but I think that's rot. I believe that most great men refuse to make the bargain with the Snakes, or with us Spiders either. They scorn Resurrection at the price demanded."

"Brother, they ain't that great," I whispered, while Beau glided on with, "However that may be, you have accepted Resurrection, sir, and so incurred an obligation which you as a gentleman must honor."

"I accepted Resurrection all right," Bruce said, a glare coming into his eyes. "When they pulled me out of my line at Passchendaele in '17 ten minutes before I died, I grabbed at the offer of life like a drunkard grabs at a drink the morning after. But even then I thought I was also seizing a chance to undo historic wrongs, work for peace." His voice was getting wilder all the time. Just beyond our circle, I noticed the New Girl watching him worshipfully. "But what did I find the Spiders wanted me for? Only to fight more wars, over and over again, make them crueler and stinkinger, cut the swath of death a little wider with each Big Change, work our way a little closer to the death of the cosmos."

Sid touched my wrist and, as Bruce raved on, he whispered to me, "What kind of ball, think you, will please and so quench this fire-brained rogue? And you love me, discover it."

I whispered back without taking my eyes off Bruce either, "I know somebody who'll be happy to put on any kind of ball he wants, if he'll just notice her."

"The New Girl, sweetling? 'Tis well. This rogue speaks like an angry angel. It touches my heart and I like it not."

Bruce was saying hoarsely but loudly, "And so we're sent on operations in the past and from each of those operations the Change Winds blow futurewards, swiftly or slowly according to the opposition they breast, sometimes rippling into each other, and any one of those Winds may shift the date of our own death ahead of the date of our Resurrection, so that in an instant—even here, outside the cosmos—we may molder and rot or crumble to dust and vanish away. The wind with our name in it may leak through the Door."

Faces hardened at that, because it's bad form to mention Change Death, and Erich flared out with, *"Halt's Maul, Kamerad!* There's always another Resurrection."

But Bruce didn't keep his mouth shut. "Is there? I know the Spiders promise it, but even if they do go back and cut another Doubleganger from my lifeline, is he me?" He slapped his chest with his bare hand. "I don't think so. And even if he is me, with unbroken consciousness, why's he been Resurrected again? Just to refight more wars and face more Change Death for the sake of an almighty power..." His voice was rising to a climax. "...an almighty power so bloody ineffectual, it can't furnish one poor Soldier pulled out of the mud of Passchendaele, one miserable Change Commando, one Godforsaken Recuperee a proper issue of equipment!"

And he held out his bare right hand toward us, fingers spread a little, as if it were the most amazing object and most deserving of outraged sympathy in the whole world.

The New Girl's timing was perfect. She whisked through us, and before he could so much as wiggle the fingers, she whipped a black gauntleted glove on it and anyone could see that it fitted his hand perfectly.

This time our laughing beat the other. We collapsed and slopped our drinks and pounded each other on the back and then started all over.

"*Ach, der Handschuh, Liebchen!* Where'd she get it?" Erich gasped in my ear.

"Probably just turned the other one inside out—that turns a left into a right—I've done it myself," I wheezed, collapsing again at the idea.

"That would put the lining outside," he objected.

"Then I don't know," I said. "We got all sorts of junk in Stores."

"It doesn't matter, *Liebchen*," he assured me. "*Ach, der Handschuh!*"

All through it, Bruce just stood there admiring the glove, moving the fingers a little now and then, and the New Girl stood watching him as if he were eating a cake she'd baked.

When the hysteria quieted down, he looked up at her with a big smile. "What did you say your name was?"

"Lili," she said, and believe you me, she was Lili to me even in my thoughts from then on, for the way she'd handled that lunatic.

"Lilian Foster," she explained. "I'm English also. Mr. Marchant, I've read *A Young Man's Fancy* I don't know how many times."

"You have? It's wretched stuff. From the Dark Ages—I mean my Cambridge days. In the trenches, I was working up some poems that were rather better."

"I won't hear you say that. But I'd be terribly thrilled to hear the new ones. Oh, Mr. Marchant, it was so strange to hear you call it Passiondale."

"Why, if I may ask?"

"Because that's the way I pronounce it to myself. But I looked it up and it's more like Pas-ken-DA-luh."

"Bless you! All the Tommies called it Passiondale, just as they called Ypres Wipers."

"How interesting. You know, Mr. Marchant, I'll wager we were Recruited in the same operation, summer of 1917. I'd got to France as a Red Cross nurse, but they found out my age and were going to send me back."

"How old were you—are you? Same thing, I mean to say."

"Seventeen."

"Seventeen in '17," Bruce murmured, his blue eyes glassy.

It was real corny dialogue and I couldn't resent the humorous leer Erich gave me as we listened to them, as if to say, "Ain't it nice, *Liebchen*, Bruce has a silly little English schoolgirl to occupy him between operations?"

Just the same, as I watched Lili in her dark bangs and pearl necklace and tight little gray dress that reached barely to her knees, and Bruce hulking over her tenderly in his snazzy hussar's rig, I knew that I was seeing the start of something that hadn't been part of me since Dave died fighting Franco years before I got on the Big Time, the sort of thing that almost made me wish there could be children in the Change World. I wondered why I'd never thought of trying to work things so that Dave got Resurrected and I told myself: no, it's all changed, I've changed, better the Change Winds don't disturb Dave or I know about it.

"No, I didn't die in 1917—I was merely Recruited then," Lili was telling Bruce. "I lived all through the Twenties, as you can see from the way I dress. But let's not talk about that, shall we? Oh, Mr. Marchant, do you think you can possibly remember any of those poems you started in the trenches? I can't fancy them bettering your sonnet that concludes with,

'The bough swings in the wind, the night is deep; Look at the stars, poor little ape, and sleep.'"

That one almost made me whoop—what monkeys we are, I thought—though I'd be the first to admit that the best line to use on a poet is one of his own—in fact, as many as possible. I decided I could safely forget our little Britons and devote myself to Erich or whatever needed me.

CHAPTER THREE
Nine for a Party

Hell is the place for me. For to Hell go the fine churchmen, and the fine knights, killed in the tourney or in some grand war, the brave soldiers and the gallant gentlemen. With them will I go. There go also the fair gracious ladies who have lovers two or three beside their lord. There go the gold and the silver, the sables and ermine. There go the harpers and the minstrels and the kings of the earth.
—Aucassin

I exchanged my drink for a new one from another tray Beau was bringing around. The gray of the Void was beginning to look real pleasant, like warm thick mist with millions of tiny diamonds floating in it. Doc was sitting grandly at the bar with a steaming tumbler of tea—a chaser, I guess, since he was just putting down a shot glass. Sid was talking to Erich and laughing at the same time and I said to myself it begins to feel like a party, but something's lacking.

It wasn't anything to do with the Major Maintainer; its telltale was glowing a steady red like a nice little home fire amid the tight cluster of dials that included all the controls except the lonely and frightening Introversion switch that was never touched. Then Maud's couch curtains winked out and there were she and the Roman sitting quietly side by side.

He looked down at his shiny boots and the rest of his black duds like he was just waking up and couldn't believe it all, and he said, "*Omnia mutantur, nos et mutamur in illis*," and I raised my eyebrows at Beau, who was taking the tray back, and he did proud by old Vicksburg by translating: "All things change and we change with them."

Then Mark slowly looked around at us, and I can testify that a Roman smile is just as warm as any other nationality, and he finally said, "We are nine, the proper number for a party. The couches, too. It is good."

Maud chuckled proudly and Erich shouted, "Welcome back from the Void, *Kamerad*," and then, because he's German and thinks all parties have to be noisy and satirically pompous, he jumped on a couch and announced, "*Herren und Damen*, permit me to introduce the noblest Roman of them all, Marcus Vipsaius Niger, legate to Nero Claudius (called Germanicus in a former time stream) and who in 763 A.U.C. (Correct, Mark? It means 10 A.D., you meatheads!) died bravely fighting the Parthians and the Snakes in the Battle of Alexandria. *Hoch, hoch, hoch!*"

We all swung our glasses and cheered with him and Sid yelled at Erich, "Keep your feet off the furniture, you unschooled rogue," and grinned and boomed at all three hussars, "Take your ease, Recuperees," and Maud and Mark got their drinks, the Roman paining Beau by refusing Falernian wine in favor of scotch and soda, and right away everyone was talking a mile a minute.

We had a lot to catch up on. There was the usual yak about the war: "The Snakes are laying mine fields in the Void," "I don't believe it, how can you mine nothing?" And the shortages—bourbon, bobby pins, and the stabilitin that would have brought Mark out of it faster—and what had become of people: "Marcia? Oh, she's not around any more," (She'd been caught in a Change Gale and green and stinking in five seconds, but I wasn't going to say that)—and Mark had to be told about Bruce's glove, which convulsed us all over again, and the Roman remembered a legionary who had carried a gripe all the way to Octavius because he'd accidentally been issued the unbelievable luxury item sugar instead of the usual salt, and Erich asked Sid if he had any new Ghostgirls in stock and Sid sucked his beard like the old goat he is. "Dost thou ask me, lusty Allemand? Nay, there are several great beauties, amongst them an Austrian countess from Strauss's Vienna, and if it were not for sweetling here... Mnnnn."

I poked a finger in Erich's chest between two of the bright buttons with their tiny death's heads. "You, my little von Hohenwald, are a menace to us real girls. You have too much of a thing about the unawakened, ghost kind."

He called me his little Demon and hugged me a bit too hard to prove it wasn't so, and then he suggested we show Bruce the Art Gallery. I thought this was a real brilliant idea, but when I tried to argue him out of it, he got stubborn. Bruce and Lili were willing to do anything anyone wanted them to, though not so willing to pay any attention while doing it. The saber cut was just a thin red line on his cheek; she'd washed away all the dried blood.

The Gallery gets you, though. It's a bunch of paintings and sculptures and especially odd knick-knacks, all made by Soldiers recuperating here, and a lot of them telling about the Change War from the stuff they're made of—brass cartridges, flaked flint, bits of ancient pottery glued into futuristic shapes, mashed-up Incan gold rebeaten by a Martian, whorls of beady Lunan wire, a picture in tempera on a crinkle-cracked thick round of quartz that had filled a starship porthole, a Sumerian inscription chiseled into a brick from an atomic oven.

There are a lot of things in the Gallery and I can always find some I haven't ever seen before. It gets you, as I say, thinking about the guys that made them and their thoughts and the far times and places they came from, and sometimes, when I'm feeling low, I'll come and look at them so I'll feel still lower and get inspired to kick myself back into a good temper. It's the only history of the Place there is and it doesn't change a great deal, because the things in it and the feelings that went into them resist the Change Winds better than anything else.

Right now, Erich's witty lecture was bouncing off the big ears I hide under my pageboy bob and I was thinking how awful it is that for us that there's not only change but Change. You don't know from one minute to the next whether a mood or idea you've got is really new or just welling up into you because the past has been altered by the Spiders or Snakes.

Change Winds can blow not only death but anything short of it, down to the featheriest fancy. They blow thousands of times faster than time moves, but no one can say how much faster or how far one of them will travel or what damage it'll do or how soon it'll damp out. The Big Time isn't the little time.

And then, for the Demons, there's the fear that our personality will just fade and someone else climb into the driver's seat and us not even know. Of course, we Demons are supposed to be able to remember through Change and in spite of it; that's why we are Demons and not Ghosts like the other Doublegangers, or merely Zombies or Unborn and nothing more, and as Beau truly said, there aren't any great men among us—and blamed few of the masses, either—we're a rare sort of people and that's why the Spiders have to Recruit us where they find us without caring about our previous knowledge and background, a Foreign Legion of time, a strange kind of folk, bright but always in the background, with built-in nostalgia and cynicism, as adaptable as Centaurian shape-changers but with memories as long as a

Lunan's six arms, a kind of Change People, you might say, the cream of the damned.

But sometimes I wonder if our memories are as good as we think they are and if the whole past wasn't once entirely different from anything we remember, and we've forgotten that we forgot.

As I say, the Gallery gets you feeling real low, and so now I said to myself, "Back to your lousy little commandant, kid," and gave myself a stiff boot.

Erich was holding up a green bowl with gold dolphins or spaceships on it and saying, "And, to my mind, this proves that Etruscan art is derived from Egyptian. Don't you agree, Bruce?"

Bruce looked up, all smiles from Lili, and said, "What was that, dear chap?"

Erich's forehead got dark as the Door and I was glad the hussars had parked their sabers along with their shakos, but before he could even get out a Jerry cussword, Doc breezed up in that plateau-state of drunkenness so like hypnotized sobriety, moving as if he were on a dolly, ghosted the bowl out of Erich's hand, said, "A beautiful specimen of Middle Systemic Venusian. When Eightaitch finished it, he told me you couldn't look at it and not feel the waves of the Northern Venusian Shallows rippling around your hoofs. But it might look better inverted. I wonder. Who are you, young officer? *Nichevo*," and he carefully put the bowl back on its shelf and rolled on.

It's a fact that Doc knows the Art Gallery better than any of us, really by heart, he being the oldest inhabitant, though he maybe picked a bad time to show off his knowledge. Erich was going to take out after him, but I said, "Nix, *Kamerad*, remember gloves and sugar," and he contented himself with complaining, "That *nichevo*—it's so gloomy and hopeless, *ungeheuerlich.* I tell you, *Liebchen*, they shouldn't have Russians working for the Spiders, not even as Entertainers."

I grinned at him and squeezed his hand. "Not much entertainment in Doc these days, is there?" I agreed.

He grinned back at me a shade sheepishly and his face smoothed and his blue eyes looked sweet again for a second and he said, "I shouldn't want to claw out at people that way, Greta, but at times I am just a jealous old man," which is not entirely true, as he isn't a day over thirty-three, although his hair is nearly white.

Our lovers had drifted on a few steps until they were almost fading into the Surgery screen. It was the last spot I would have picked for the formal preliminaries to a little British smooching, but Lili probably didn't share my prejudices, though I remembered she'd told me she'd served a brief hitch in an Arachnoid Field Hospital before being transferred to the Place.

But she couldn't have had anything like the experience I'd had during my short and sour career as a Spider nurse, when I'd acquired my best-hated nightmare and flopped completely (jobwise, but on the floor, too) at seeing a doctor flick a switch and a being, badly injured but human, turn into a long cluster of glistening strange fruit—ugh, it always makes me want to toss my cookies and my buttons. And to think that dear old Daddy Anton wanted his Greta chile to be a doctor.

Well, I could see this wasn't getting me anywhere I wanted to go, and after all there was a party going on.

Doc was babbling something at a great rate to Sid—I just hoped Doc wouldn't get inspired to go into his animal imitations, which sound pretty fierce and once seriously offended some recuperating ETs.

Maud was demonstrating to Mark a 23rd Century two-step and Beau sat down at the piano and improvised softly on her rhythm.

As the deep-thrumming relaxing notes hit us, Erich's face brightened and he dragged me over. Pleasantly soon I had my feet off the diamond-rough floor, which we don't carpet because most of the ETs, the dear boys, like it hard, and I was shouldering back deep into the couch nearest the piano, with cushions all around me and a fresh drink in my hand, while my Nazi boy friend was getting ready to discharge his *Weltschmerz* as song, which didn't alarm me too much, as his baritone is passable.

Things felt real good, like the Maintainer was just idling to keep the Place in existence and moored to the cosmos, not exerting itself at all or at most taking an occasional lazy paddle stroke. At times the Place's loneliness can be happy and comfortable.

Then Beau raised an eyebrow at Erich, who nodded, and next thing they were launched into a song we all know, though I've never found out where it originally came from. This time it made me think of Lili, and I wondered why—and why it's a tradition at Recuperation Stations to call the new girl Lili, though in this case it happened to be her real name.

Standing in the Doorway just outside of space, Winds of Change blow 'round you but don't touch your face; You smile as you whisper tenderly, "Please cross to me, Recuperee; The operation's over, come in and close the Door."

CHAPTER FOUR
S.O.S. from Nowhere

De Bailhache, Fresca, Mrs. Cammel, whirled Beyond the circuit of the shuddering Bear In fractured atoms.
—*Eliot*

I realized the piano had deserted Erich and I cranked my head up and saw Beau, Maud and Sid streaking for the control divan. The Major Maintainer was blinking emergency-green and fast, but the code was plain enough for even me to recognize the Spider distress call and for a second I felt just sick. Then Erich blew out his reserve breath in the middle of "Door" and I gave myself another of those helpful mental boots at the base of the spine and we hurried after them toward the center of the Place along with Mark.

The blinks faded as we got there and Sid told us not to move because we were making shadows. He glued an eye to the telltale and we held still as statues as he caressed the dials like he was making love.

One sensitive hand flicked out past the Introversion switch over to the Minor Maintainer and right away the Place was dark as your soul and there was nothing for me but Erich's arm and the knowledge that Sid was nursing a green light I couldn't even see, although my eyes had plenty time to accommodate.

Then the green light finally came back very slowly and I could see the dear reliable old face—the green-gold beard making him look like a merman—and then the telltale flared bright and Sid flicked on the Place lights and I leaned back.

"That nails them, lads, whoever and whenever they may be. Get ready for a pick-up."

Beau, who was closest of course, looked at him sharply. Sid shrugged uneasily. "Meseemed at first it was from our own globe a thousand years before our Lord, but that indication flickered and faded like witchfire. As it is, the call comes from something smaller than the Place and certes adrift from the cosmos. Meseemed too at one point I knew the fist of the caller—an antipodean atomicist named Benson-Carter—but that likewise changed."

Beau said, "We're not in the right phase of the cosmos-Places rhythm for a pick-up, are we, sir?"

Sid answered, "Ordinarily not, boy."

Beau continued, "I didn't think we had any pick-ups scheduled. Or stand-by orders."

Sid said, "We haven't."

Mark's eyes glowed. He tapped Erich on the shoulder. "An octavian denarius against ten Reichsmarks it is a Snake trap."

Erich's grin showed his teeth. "Make it first through the Door next operation and I'm on."

It didn't take that to tell me things were serious, or the thought that there's always a first time for bumping into something from really outside the cosmos. The Snakes have broken our code more than once. Maud was quietly serving out weapons and Doc was helping her. Only Bruce and Lili stood off. But they were watching.

The telltale brightened. Sid reached toward the Maintainer, saying, "All right, my hearties. Remember, through this Doorway pass the fishiest finaglers in and out of the cosmos."

The Door appeared to the left and above where it should be and darkened much too fast. There was a gust of stale salt seawind, if that makes sense, but no stepped-up Change Winds I could tell—and I had been bracing myself against them. The Door got inky and there was a flicker of gray fur whips and a flash of copper flesh and gilt and something dark and a clump of hoofs and Erich was sighting a stun gun across his left forearm, and then the Door had vanished like that and a tentacled silvery Lunan and a Venusian satyr were coming straight toward us.

The Lunan was hugging a pile of clothes and weapons. The satyr was helping a wasp-waisted woman carry a heavy-looking bronze chest. The woman was wearing a short skirt and high-collared bolero jacket of leather so dark brown it was almost black. She had a two-horned *petsofa* hairdress and she was boldly gilded here and there and wore sandals and copper anklets and wristlets—one of them a copper-plated

Caller—and from her wide copper belt hung a short-handled double-headed ax. She was dark-complexioned and her forehead and chin receded, but the effect was anything but weak; she had a face like a beautiful arrowhead—and a familiar one, by golly!

But before I could say, "Kabysia Labrys," Maud shrilly beat me to it with, "It's Kaby with two friends. Break out a couple of Ghostgirls."

And then I saw it really was old-home week because I recognized my Lunan boy friend Ilhilihis, and in the midst of all the confusion I got a nice kick out of knowing I was getting so I could tell the personality of one silver-furred muzzle from another.

They reached the control divan and Illy dumped his load and the others let down the chest, and Kaby staggered but shook off the two ETs when they started to support her, and she looked daggers at Sid when he tried to do the same, although she's his "sweet Keftian friend" he'd mentioned to Bruce.

She leaned straight-armed on the divan and took two gasping breaths so deep that the ridges of her spine showed through her brown-skinned waist, and then she threw up her head and commanded, "Wine!"

While Beau was rushing it, Sid tried to take her hand again, saying, "Sweetling, I'd never heard you call before and knew not this pretty little fist," but she ripped out, "Save your comfort for the Lunan," and I looked and saw—Hey, Zeus!— that one of Ilhilihis' six tentacles was lopped off halfway.

That was for me, and, going to him, I fast briefed myself: "Remember, he only weighs fifty pounds for all he's seven feet high; he doesn't like low sounds or to be grabbed; the two legs aren't tentacles and don't act the same; uses them for long walks, tentacles for leaps; uses tentacles for close vision too and for manipulation, of course; extended, they mean he's at ease; retracted, on guard or nervous; sharply retracted, disgusted; greeting—"

Just then, one of them swept across my face like a sweet-smelling feather duster and I said, "Illy, man, it's been a lot of sleeps," and brushed my fingers across his muzzle. It still took a little self-control not to hug him, and I did reach a little cluckingly for his lopped tentacle, but he wafted it away from me and the little voice-box belted to his side squeaked, "Naughty, naughty. Papa will fix his little old self. Greta girl, ever bandaged even a Terra octopus?"

I had, an intelligent one from around a quarter billion A.D., but I didn't tell him so. I stood and let him talk to the palm of my hand with one of his tentacles—I don't savvy feather-talk but it feels good, though I've often wondered who taught him English—and watched him use a couple others to whisk a sort of Lunan band-aid out of his pouch and cap his wound with it.

Meanwhile, the satyr knelt over the bronze chest, which was decorated with little death's heads and crosses with hoops at the top and swastikas, but looking much older than Nazi, and the satyr said to Sid, "Quick thinkin, Gov, when ya saw the Door comin in high n soffened up gravty unner it, but cud I hav sum hep now?"

Sid touched the Minor Maintainer and we all got very light and my stomach did a flip-flop while the satyr piled on the chest the clothes and weapons that Illy had been carrying and pranced off with it all and carefully put it down at the end of the bar. I decided the satyr's English instructor must have been quite a character, too. Wish I'd met him—her—it.

Sid thought to ask Illy if he wanted Moon-normal gravity in one sector, but my boy likes to mix, and being such a lightweight, Earth-normal gravity doesn't bother him. As he said to me once, "Would Jovian gravity bother a beetle, Greta girl?"

I asked Illy about the satyr and he squeaked that his name was Sevensee and that he'd never met him before this operation. I knew the satyrs were from a billion years in the future, just as the Loonies were from a billion in the past, and I thought—Kreesed us!—but it must have been a real big or emergency-like operation to have the Spiders using those two for it, with two billion years between them—a time-difference that gives you a feeling of awe for a second, you know.

I started to ask Illy about it, but just then Beau came scampering back from the bar with a big red-and-black earthenware goblet of wine—we try to keep a variety of drinking tools in stock so folks will feel more at home. Kaby grabbed it from him and drained most of it in one swallow and then smashed it on the floor. She does things like that, though Sid's tried to teach her better. Then she stared at what she was thinking about until the whites showed all around her eyes and her lips pulled way back from her teeth and she looked a lot less human than the two ETs, just like a fury. Only a time traveler knows how like the wild murals and engravings of them some of the ancients can look.

My hair stood up at the screech she let out. She smashed a fist into the divan and cried, "Goddess! Must I see Crete destroyed, revived, and now destroyed again? It is too much for your servant."

Personally, I thought she could stand anything.

There was a rush of questions at what she said about Crete—I asked one of them, for the news certainly frightened me—but she shot up her arm straight for silence and took a deep breath and began.

"In the balance hung the battle. Rowing like black centipedes, the Dorian hulls bore down on our outnumbered ships. On the bright beach, masked by rocks, Sevensee and I stood by the needle gun, ready to give the black hulls silent wounds. Beside us was Ilhilihis, suited as a sea monster. But then…then…"

Then I saw she wasn't altogether the iron babe, for her voice broke and she started to shake and to sob rackingly, although her face was still a mask of rage, and she threw up the wine. Sid stepped in and made her stop, which I think he'd been wanting to do all along.

CHAPTER FIVE
Sid Insists on Ghostgirls

Whenever I take up a newspaper and read it, I fancy I see ghosts creeping between the lines. There must be ghosts all over the world. They must be as countless as the grains of the sands, it seems to me.
—Ibsen

My Elizabethan boy friend put his fists on his hips and laid down the law to us as if we were a lot of nervous children who'd been playing too hard.

"Look you, masters, this is a Recuperation Station and I am running it as such. A plague of all operations! I care not if the frame of things disjoints and the whole Change World goes to ruin, but you, warrior maid, are going to rest and drink more wine slowly before you tell your tale and your colleagues are going to be properly companioned. No questions, anyone. Beau, and you love us, give us a lively tune."

Kaby relaxed a little and let him put his hand carefully against her back in token of support and she said grudgingly, "All right, Fat Belly."

Then, so help me, to the tune of the Muskrat Ramble, which I'd taught Beau, we got girls for those two ETs and everybody properly paired up.

Right here I want to point out that a lot of the things they say in the Change World about Recuperation Stations simply aren't so—and anyway they always leave out nine-tenths of it. The Soldiers that come through the Door are looking for a good time, sure, but they're hurt real bad too, every one of them, deep down in their minds and hearts, if not always in their bodies or so you can see it right away.

Believe me, a temporal operation is no joke, and to start with, there isn't one person in a hundred who can endure to be cut from his lifeline and become a really wide-awake Doubleganger—a Demon, that is—let alone a Soldier. What does a badly hurt and mixed-up creature need who's been fighting hard? *One individual* to look out for him and feel for him and patch him up, and it helps if the one is of the opposite sex—that's something that goes beyond species.

There's your basis for the Place and the wild way it goes about its work, and also for most other Recuperation Stations or Entertainment Spots. The name Entertainer can be misleading, but I like it. She's got to be a lot more than a good party girl—or boy—though she's got to be that too. She's got to be a nurse and a psychologist and an actress and a mother and a practical ethnologist and a lot of things with longer names—and a reliable friend.

None of us are all those things perfectly or even near it. We just try. But when the call comes, Entertainers have to forget grudges and gripes and envies and jealousies—and remember, they're lively people with sharp emotions— because there isn't any time then for anything but *help and don't ask who*!

And, deep inside her, a good Entertainer doesn't care who. Take the way it shaped up this time. It was pretty clear to me I ought to shift to Illy, although I wasn't quite easy in my mind about leaving Erich, because the Lunan was a long time from home and, after all, Erich was among anthropoids. Ilhilihis needed someone who was *simpatico*.

I like Illy and not just because he is a sort of tall cross between a spider monkey and a persian cat—though that is a handsome combo when you come to think of it. I like him for himself. So when he came in all lopped and shaky after a mean operation, I was the right person to look out for him. Now I've made my little speech and know-nothings in the Change World can go on making their bum jokes. But I ask you, how could an arrangement between Illy and me be anything but Platonic?

We might have had some octopoid girls and nymphs in stock—Sid couldn't be sure until he checked—but Ilhilihis and Sevensee voted for real people and I knew Sid saw it their way. Maud squeezed Mark's hand and tripped over to Sevensee ("Those are sharp hoofs you got, man." She's picked up some of my language, like she has everything else), though Beau did frown over his shoulder at Lili from the piano, maybe to argue that she ought to take on the ET, as Mark had been a real casualty and could use live nursing. But it was plain as day to anybody but Beau that Bruce and Lili were a big thing and the last to be disturbed.

Erich acted stiffly hurt at losing me, but I knew he wasn't. He thinks he has a great technique with Ghostgirls and he likes to show it off, and he really is pretty slick at it, if you go for that sort of thing and—yang my yin!—who doesn't at times?

And when Sid formally wafted the Countess out of Stores—a real blonde stunner in a white satin hobble skirt with a white egret swaying up from her tiny hat, way ahead of Maud and Lili and me when it came to looks, though transparent as cigarette smoke—and when Erich clicked his heels and bowed over her hand and proudly conducted her to a couch, black Svengali to her Trilby, and started to German-talk some life into her with much head cocking and toothy smiling and a steady flow of witty flattery, and when she began to flirt back and the dream-like look in her eyes sharpened hungrily and focused on him—well, then I knew that Erich was happy and felt he was doing proud by the *Reichswehr*. No, my little commandant wasn't worrying me on that score.

Mark had drawn a Greek hetaera, name of Phryne; I suppose not the one who maybe still does the famous courtroom striptease back in Athens, and he was waking her up with little sips of his scotch and soda, though, from some looks he'd flashed, I got the idea Kaby was the kid he really went for. Sid was coaxing the fighting gal to take some high-energy bread and olives along with the wine, and, for a wonder, Doc seemed to be carrying on an animated and rational conversation with Sevensee and Maud, maybe comparing notes on the Northern Venusian Shallows, and Beau had got on to Panther Rag, and Bruce and Lili were leaning on the piano, smiling very appreciatively, but talking to each other a mile a minute.

Illy turned back from inspecting them all and squeaked, "Animals with clothes are so refreshing, dahling! Like you're all carrying banners!"

Maybe he had something there, though my banners were kind of Ash Wednesday, a charcoal gray sweater and skirt. He looked at my mouth with a tentacle to see how I was smiling and he squeaked softly, "Do I seem somewhat dull and commonplace to you, Greta girl, because I haven't got banners? Just another Zombie from a billion years or more in your past, as gray and lifeless as Luna is today, not as when she was a real dreamy sister planet simply bursting with air and water and feather forests. Or am I as strangely interesting to you as you are to me, girl from a billion years in my future?"

"Illy, you're sweet," I told him, giving him a little pat. I noticed his fur was still vibrating nervously and I decided the heck with Sid's orders, I'm going to pump him about what he was doing with Kaby and the satyr. Couldn't have him a billion years from home and bottled up, too. Besides, I was curious.

CHAPTER SIX
Crete, Circa 1300 B.C.

Maiden, Nymph, and Mother are the eternal royal Trinity of the island, and the Goddess, who is worshipped there in each of these aspects, as New Moon, Full Moon, and Old Moon, is the sovereign Deity.
—*Graves*

Kaby pushed back at Sid some seconds of bread and olives, and, when he raised his bushy eyebrows, gave him a curt nod that meant she knew what she was doing. She stood up and sort of took a position. All the talk quieted down fast, even Bruce's and Lili's. Kaby's face and voice weren't strained now, but they weren't relaxed either.

"Woe to Spider! Woe to Cretan! Heavy is the news I bring you. Bear it bravely, like strong women. When we got the gun unlimbered, I heard seaweed fry and crackle. We three leaped behind the rock wall, saw our gun grow white as sunlight in a heat-ray of the Serpents! Natch, we feared we were outnumbered and I called upon my Caller."

I don't know how she does it, but she does—in English too. That is, when she figures she's got something important to report, and maybe she needs a little time to get ready.

Beau claims that all the ancients fit their thoughts into measured lines as naturally as we pick a word that will do, but I'm not sure how good the Vicksburg language department is. Though why I should wonder about things like that when I've got Kaby spouting the stuff right in front of me, I don't know.

"But I didn't die there, kiddos. I still hoped to hurt the Greek ships, maybe with the Snake's own heat gun. So I quick tried to outflank them. My two comrades crawled beside me—they are males, but they have courage. Soon we spied the ambush-setters. They were Snakes and they were many, filthily disguised as Cretans."

There was an indignant murmur at this, for our cutthroat Change War has its code, the Soldiers tell me. Being an Entertainer, I don't have to say what I think.

"They had seen us when we saw them," Kaby swept on, "and they loosed a killing volley. Heat- and knife-rays struck about us in a storm of wind and fire, and the Lunan lost a feeler, fighting for Crete's Triple Goddess. So we dodged behind a sand hill, steered our flight back toward the water. It was awful, what we saw there: Crete's brave ships all sunk or sinking, blue sky sullied by their death-smoke. Once again the Greeks had licked us!—aided by the filthy Serpents.

"Round our wrecks, their black ships scurried, like black beetles, filth their diet, yet this day they dine on heroes. On the quiet sunlit beach there, I could feel a Change Gale blowing, working changes deep inside me, aches and pains that were a stranger's. Half my memories were doubled, half my lifeline crooked and twisted, three new moles upon my sword-hand. Goddess, Goddess, Triple Goddess—"

Her voice wavered and Sid reached out a hand, but she straightened her back.

"Triple Goddess, give me courage to tell everything that happened. We ran down into the water, hoping to escape by diving. We had hardly gotten under when the heat-rays hit above us, turning all the cool green surface to a roaring white inferno. But as I believe I told you, I was calling on my Caller, and a Door now opened to us, deep below the deadly steam-clouds. We dived in like frightened minnows and a lot of water with us."

Off Chicago's Gold Coast, Dave once gave me a lesson in skin-diving and, remembering it, I got a flash of Kaby's Door in the dark depths.

"For a moment, all was chaos. Then the Door slammed shut behind us. We'd been picked up in time's nick by—an Express Room of our Spiders!—sloshing two feet deep in water, much more cramped for space than this Place. It was manned by a magician, an old coot named Benson-Carter. He dispelled the water quickly and reported on his Caller. We'd got dry, were feeling human, Illy here had shed his swimsuit, when we looked at the Maintainer. It was glowing, changing, melting! And when Benson-Carter touched it, he fell backward—death was in him. Then the Void began to darken, narrow, shrink and close around us, so I called upon my Caller—without wasting time, let me tell you!

"We can't say for sure what was it slowly squeezed that sweet Express Room, but we fear the dirty Snakes have found a way to find our Places and attack outside the cosmos!— found the Spiderweb that links us in the Void's gray less-than-nothing."

No murmur this time. This reaction was genuine; we'd been hit where we lived and I could see everybody was scared as sick as I was. Except maybe Bruce and Lili, who were still holding hands and beaming gently. I decided they were the kind that love makes brave, which it doesn't do to me. It just gives me two people to worry about.

"I can see you dig our feelings," Kaby continued. "This thing scared the pants off of us. If we could have, we'd have even Introverted the Maintainer, broken all the ties that bind us, chanced it incommunicado. But the little old Maintainer was a seething red-hot puddle filled with bubbles big as handballs. We sat tight and watched the Void close. I kept calling on my Caller."

I squeezed my eyes shut, but that made it easier to see the three of them with the Void shutting down on them. (Was ours still behaving? Yes, Bibi Miriam.) Poetry or no poetry, it got me.

"Benson-Carter, lying dying, also thought the Snakes had done it. And he knew that death was in him, so he whispered me his mission, giving me precise instructions: how to press the seven death's hands, starting lockside counterclockwise, one, three, five, six, two, four, seven, then you have a half an hour; after you have pressed the seven, do not monkey with the buttons—get out fast and don't stop moving."

I wasn't getting this part and I couldn't see that anyone else was, though Bruce was whispering to Lili. I remembered seeing skulls engraved on the bronze chest. I looked at Illy and he nodded a tentacle and spread two to say, I guessed, that yes, Benson-Carter had said something like that, but no, Illy didn't know much about it.

"All these things and more he whispered," Kaby went on, "with the last gasps of his life-force, telling all his secret orders—for he'd not been sent to get us, he was on a separate mission, when he heard my SOSs. Sid, it's you he was to contact, as the first leg of his mission, pick up from you three black hussars, death's-head Demons, daring Soldiers, then to wait until the Places next match rhythm with the cosmos— matter of two mealtimes, barely—and to tune in northern Egypt in the age of the last Caesar, in the year of Rome's swift downfall, there to start an operation in a battle near a city named for Thrace's Alexander, there to change the course of battle, blow sky-high the stinking Serpents, all their agents, all their Zombies!

"Goddess, pardon, now I savvy how you've guided my least footstep, when I thought you'd gone and left me—for I flubbed your three-mole signal. We've found Sid's Place, that's the first leg, and I see the three black hussars, and we've brought with us the weapon and the Parthian disguises, salvaged from the doomed Express Room when your Door appeared in time's nick, and the Room around us closing spewed us through before it vanished with the corpse of Benson-Carter. Triple Goddess, draw the milk now from the womanhood I flaunt here and inject the blackest hatred! Vengeance now upon the Serpents, vengeance sweet in northern Egypt, for your island, Crete, Goddess!—and a victory for the Spiders! Goddess, Goddess, we can swing it!"

The roar that made me try to stop my ears with my shoulders didn't come from Kaby—she'd spoken her piece—but from Sid. The dear boy was purple enough to make me want to remind him you can die of high blood pressure just as easy in the Change World.

"Dump me with ops! 'Sblood, I'll not endure it! Is this a battle post? They'll be mounting operations from field hospitals next. Kabysia Labrys, thou art mad to suggest it. And what's this prattle of locks, clocks, and death's heads, buttons and monkeys? This brabble, this farrago, this hocus-pocus! And where's the weapon you prate of? In that whoreson bronze casket, I suppose."

She nodded, looking blank and almost a little shy as poetic possession faded from her. Her answer came like its faltering last echo.

"It is nothing but a tiny tactical atomic bomb."

CHAPTER SEVEN
Time to Think

After about 0.1 millisecond (one ten-thousandth part of a second) has elapsed, the radius of the ball of fire is some 45 feet, and the temperature is then in the vicinity of 300,000 degrees Centigrade. At this instant, the luminosity, as observed at a distance of 100,000 yards (5.7 miles), is approximately 100 times that of the sun as seen at the earth's surface...the ball of fire expands very rapidly to its maximum radius of 450 feet within less than a second from the explosion.
—*Los Alamos*

Brother, that was all we needed to make everybody but Kaby and the two ETs start yelping at once, me included. It may seem strange that Change People, able to whiz through time and space and roust around outside the cosmos and knowing at least by hearsay of weapons a billion years in the future, like the Mindbomb, should panic at being shut in with a little primitive mid-20th Century gadget. Well, they feel the same as atomic scientists would feel if a Bengal tiger were brought into their laboratory, neither more nor less scared.

I'm a moron at physics, but I do know the Fireball is bigger than the Place. Remember that, besides the bomb, we'd recently been presented with a lot of other fears we hadn't had time to cope with, especially the business of the Snakes having learned how to get at our Places and melt the Maintainers and collapse them. Not to mention the general impression—first Saint Petersburg, then Crete—that the whole Change War was going against the Spiders.

Yet, in a free corner of my mind, I was shocked at how badly we were all panicking. It made me admit what I didn't like to: that we were all in pretty much the same state as Doc, except that the bottle didn't happen to be our out.

And had the rest of us been controlling our drinking so well lately?

Maud yelled, "Jettison it!" and pulled away from the satyr and ran from the bronze chest. Beau, harking back to what they'd thought of doing in the Express Room when it was too late, hissed, "Sirs, we must Introvert," and vaulted over the piano bench and legged it for the control divan. Erich seconded him with a white-faced "*Gott in Himmel, ja!*" from beside the surly, forgotten Countess, holding, by its slim stem, an empty, rose-stained wine glass.

I felt my mind flinch, because Introverting a Place is several degrees worse than foxholing. It's supposed not only to keep the Door tight shut, but also to lock it so even the Change Winds can't get through—cut the Place loose from the cosmos altogether.

I'd never talked with anyone from a Place that had been Introverted.

Mark dumped Phryne off his lap and ran after Maud. The Greek Ghostgirl, quite solid now, looked around with sleepy fear and fumbled her apple-green chiton together at the throat. She wrenched my attention away from everyone else for a moment, and I couldn't help wondering whether the person or Zombie back in the cosmos, from whose lifeline the Ghost has been taken, doesn't at least have strange dreams or thoughts when something like this happens.

Sid stopped Beau, though he almost got bowled over doing it, and he held the gambler away from the Maintainer in a bear hug and bellowed over his shoulders, "Masters, are you mad? Have you lost your wits? Maud! Mark! Marcus! Magdalene! On your lives, unhand that casket!"

Maud had swept the clothes and bows and quivers and stuff off it and was dragging it out from the bar toward the

Door sector, so as to dump it through fast when we got one, I guess, while Mark acted as if he were trying to help her and wrestle it away from her at the same time.

They kept on as if they hadn't heard a word Sid said, with Mark yelling, "Let go, *meretrix*! This holds Rome's answer to Parthia on the Nile."

Kaby watched them as if she wanted to help Mark but scorned to scuffle with a mere—well, Mark had said it in Latin, I guess—call girl.

Then, on the top of the bronze chest, I saw those seven lousy skulls starting at the lock as plain as if they'd been under a magnifying glass, though ordinarily they'd have been a vague circle to my eyes at the distance, and I lost my mind and started to run in the opposite direction, but Illy whipped three tentacles around me, gentle-like, and squeaked, "Easy now, Greta girl, don't you be doing it, too. Hold still or Papa spank. My, my, but you two-leggers can whirl about when you have a mind to."

My stampede had carried his featherweight body a couple of yards, but it stopped me and I got my mind back, partly.

"Unhand it, I say!" Sid repeated without accomplishing anything, and he released Beau, though he kept a hand near the gambler's shoulder.

Then my fat friend from Lynn Regis looked real distraught at the Void and blustered at no one in particular, "'Sdeath, think you I'd mutiny against my masters, desert the Spiders, go to ground like a spent fox and pull my hole in after me? A plague of such cowardice! Who suggests it? Introversion's no mere last-ditch device. Unless ordered, supervised and sanctioned, it means the end. And what if I'd Introverted ere we got Kaby's call for succor, hey?"

His warrior maid nodded with harsh approval and he noticed it and shook his free hand at her and scolded her, "Not that I say yea to your mad plan for that Devil's casket, you half-clad lackwit. And yet to jettison... Oh, ye gods, ye gods..." He wiped his hand across his face. "...grant me a minute in which I may think!"

Thinking time wasn't an item even on the strictly limited list at the moment, although Sevensee, squatting dourly on his hairy haunches where Maud had left him, threw in a dead-pan "Thas tellin em, Gov."

Then Doc at the bar stood up tall as Abe Lincoln in his top hat and shawl and 19th Century duds and raised an unwavering arm for silence and said something that sounded like: "Introversh, inversh, glovsh," and then his enunciation switched to better than perfect as he continued, "I know to an absolute certainty what we must do."

It showed me how rabbity we were that the Place got quiet as a church while we all stopped whatever we were doing and waited breathless for a poor drunk to tell us how to save ourselves.

He said something like, "Inversh...bosh..." and held our eyes for a moment longer. Then the light went out of his and he slobbered out a "*Nichevo*" and slid an arm far along the bar for a bottle and started to pour it down his throat without stopping sliding.

Before he completed his collapse to the floor, in the split second while our attention was still focused on the bar, Bruce vaulted up on top of it, so fast it was almost like he'd popped up from nowhere, though I'd seen him start from behind the piano.

"I've a question. Has anyone here triggered that bomb?" he said in a voice that was very clear and just loud enough. "So it can't go off," he went on after just the right pause, his easy grin and brisk manner putting more heart into me all the time. "What's more, if it were to be triggered, we'd still have half an hour. I believe you said it had that long a fuse?"

He stabbed a finger at Kaby. She nodded.

"Right," he said. "It'd have to be that long for whoever plants it in the Parthian camp to get away. There's another safety margin.

"Second question. Is there a locksmith in the house?"

For all Bruce's easiness, he was watching us like a golden eagle and he caught Beau's and Maud's affirmatives before they had a chance to explain or hedge them and said, "That's very good. Under certain circumstances, you two'd be the ones to go to work on the chest. But before we consider that, there's Question Three: Is anyone here an atomics technician?"

That one took a little conversation to straighten out, Illy having to explain that, yes, the Early Lunans had atomic power—hadn't they blasted the life off their planet with it and made all those ghastly craters?—but no, he wasn't a technician exactly, he was a "thinger" (I thought at first his squeakbox was lisping); what was a thinger?—well, a thinger was someone who manipulated things in a way that was truly impossible to describe, but no, you couldn't possibly thing atomics; the idea was quite ridiculous, so he couldn't be an atomics thinger; the term was worse than a contradiction, well, really!—while Sevensee, from his two-thousand-millennia advantage of the Lunan, grunted to the effect that his culture didn't rightly use any kind of power, but just sort of moved satyrs and stuff by wrastling space-time around, "or think em roun ef we hafta. Can't think em in the Void, tho, wus luck. Hafta have—I dunno wut. Dun havvit anyhow."

"So we don't have an A-tech," Bruce summed up, "which makes it worse than useless, downright dangerous, to tamper with the chest. We wouldn't know what to do if we did get inside safely. One more question." He directed it toward Sid. "How long before we can jettison anything?"

Sid, looking a shade jealous, yet mostly grateful for the way Bruce had calmed his chickens, started to explain, but Bruce didn't seem to be taking any chance of losing his audience, and as soon as Sid got to the word "rhythm," he pulled the answer away from him.

"In brief, not until we can effectively tune in on the cosmos again. Thank you, Master Lessingham. That's at least five hours—two mealtimes, as the Cretan officer put it," and he threw Kaby a quick soldierly smile. "So, whether the bomb goes to Egypt or elsewhere, there's not a thing we can do about it for five hours. All right then!"

His smile blinked out like a light and he took a couple of steps up and down the bar, as if measuring the space he had. Two or three cocktail glasses sailed off and popped, but he didn't seem to notice them and we hardly did either. It was creepy the way he kept staring from one to another of us. We had to look up. Behind his face, with the straight golden hair flirting around it, was only the Void.

"All right then," he repeated suddenly. "We're twelve Spiders and two Ghosts, and we've time for a bit of a talk, and we're all in the same bloody boat, fighting the same bloody war, so we'll all know what we're talking about. I raised the subject a while back, but I was steamed up about a glove, and it was a big jest. All right! But now the gloves are off!"

Bruce ripped them out of his belt where they'd been tucked and slammed them down on the bar, to be kicked off the next time he paced back and forth, and it wasn't funny.

"Because," he went right on, "I've been getting a completely new picture of what this Spiders' war has been doing to each one of us. Oh, it's jolly good sport to slam around in space and time and then have a rugged little party outside both of them when the operation's over. It's sweet to know there's no cranny of reality so narrow, no privacy so intimate or sacred, no wall of was or will be strong enough, that we can't shoulder in. Knowledge is a glamorous thing, sweeter than lust or gluttony or the passion of fighting and including all three, the ultimate insatiable hunger, and it's great to be Faust, even in a pack of other Fausts.

"It's sweet to jigger reality, to twist the whole course of a man's life or a culture's, to ink out his or its past and scribble in a new one, and be the only one to know and gloat over the changes—hah! killing men or carrying off women isn't in it for glutting the sense of power. It's sweet to feel the Change Winds blowing through you and know the pasts that were and the past that is and the pasts that may be. It's sweet to wield the Atropos and cut a Zombie or Unborn out of his lifeline and look the Doubleganger in the face and see the Resurrection-glow in it and Recruit a brother, welcome a newborn fellow Demon into our ranks and decide whether he'll best fit as Soldier, Entertainer, or what.

"Or he can't stand Resurrection, it fries or freezes him, and you've got to decide whether to return him to his lifeline and his Zombie dreams, only they'll be a little grayer and horrider than they were before, or whether, if she's got that tantalizing something, to bring her shell along for a Ghostgirl—that's sweet, too. It's even sweet to have Change Death poised over your neck, to know that the past isn't the precious indestructible thing you've been taught it was, to know that there's no certainty about the future either, whether there'll even be one, to know that no part of reality is holy, that the cosmos itself may wink out like a flicked switch and God be not and nothing left but nothing!"

He threw out his arms against the Void. "And knowing all that, it's doubly sweet to come through the Door into the Place and be out of the worst of the Change Winds and enjoy a well-earned Recuperation and share the memories of all these sweetnesses I've been talking about, and work out all the fascinating feelings you've been accumulating back in the cosmos, layer by black layer, in the company of and with the help of the best bloody little band of fellow Fausts and Faustines going!

"Oh, it's a sweet life, all right, but I'm asking you…" And here his eyes stabbed us again, one by one, fast, "…I'm asking you what it's done to us. I've been getting a completely new picture, as I said, of what my life was and what it could have been if there'd been changes of the sort that even we Demons can't make, and what my life is. I've been watching how we've all been responding to things just now, to the news of Saint Petersburg and to what the Cretan officer told beautifully—only it wasn't beautiful what she had to tell—and mostly to that bloody box of bomb. And I'm simply asking each one of you, what's happened to you?"

He stopped his pacing and stuck his thumbs in his belt and seemed to be listening to the wheels turning in at least eleven other heads—only I stopped mine pretty quick, with Dave and Father and the Rape of Chicago coming up out of the dark on the turn and Mother and the Indiana Dunes and Jazz Limited just behind them, followed by the unthinkable thing the Spider doctor had flicked into existence when I flopped as a nurse, because I can't stand that to be done to my mind by anybody but myself.

I stopped them by using the old infallible Entertainers' gimmick, a fast survey of the most interesting topic there is— other people's troubles.

Offhand, Beau looked as if he had most troubles, shamed by his boss and his girl given her heart to a Soldier; he was hugging them to himself very quiet.

I didn't stop for the two ETs—they're too hard to figure— or for Doc; nobody can tell whether a fallen-down drunk's at the black or bright end of his cycle; you just know it's cycling.

Maud ought to be suffering as much as Beau, called names and caught out in a panic, which always hurts her because she's plus three hundred years more future than the rest of us and figures she ought to be that much wiser, which she isn't always—not to mention she's over fifty years old, though her home-century cosmetic science keeps her looking and acting teenage most of the time. She'd backed away from the bronze chest so as not to stand out, and now Lili came from behind the piano and stood beside her.

Lili had the opposite of troubles, a great big glow for Bruce, proud as a promised princess watching her betrothed. Erich frowned when he saw her, for he seemed proud too, proud of the way his *Kamerad* had taken command of us panicky whacks *Führer*-fashion. Sid still looked mostly grateful and inclined to let Bruce keep on talking.

Even Kaby and Mark, those two dragons hot for battle, standing a little in front and to one side of us by the bronze chest, like its guardians, seemed willing to listen. They made me realize one reason Sid had for letting Bruce run on, although the path his talk was leading us down was flashing with danger signals: When it was over, there'd still be the problem of what to do with the bomb, and a real opposition shaping up between Soldiers and Entertainers, and Sid was hoping a solution would turn up in the meantime or at least was willing to put off the evil day.

But beyond all that, and like the rest of us, I could tell from the way Sid was squinting his browy eyes and chewing his beardy lip that he was shaken and moved by what Bruce had said. This New Boy had dipped into our hearts and counted our kicks so beautifully, better than most of us could have done, and then somehow turned them around so that we had to think of what messes and heels and black sheep and lost lambs we were—well, we wanted to keep on listening.

CHAPTER EIGHT
A Place to Stand

Give me a place to stand, and I will move the world.
—Archimedes

Bruce's voice had a faraway touch and he was looking up left at the Void as he said, "Have you ever really wondered why the two sides of this war are called the Snakes and the Spiders? Snakes may be clear enough—you always call the enemy something dirty. But Spiders—our name for ourselves? Bear with me, Ilhilihis; I know that no being is created dirty or malignant by Nature, but this is a matter of anthropoid feelings and folkways. Yes, Mark, I know that some of your legions have nicknames like the Drunken Lions and the Snails, and that's about as insulting as calling the British Expeditionary Force the Old Contemptibles.

"No, you'd have to go to bands of vicious youths in cities slated for ruin to find a habit of naming like ours, and even they would try to brighten up the black a bit. But simply— Spiders. And Snakes, for that's their name for themselves too, you know. Spiders and Snakes. What are our masters, that we give them names like that?"

It gave me the shivers and set my mind working in a dozen directions and I couldn't stop it, although it made the shivers worse.

Illy beside me now—I'd never given it a thought before, but he did have eight legs of a sort, and I remembered thinking of him as a spider monkey, and hadn't the Lunans had wisdom and atomic power and a billion years in which to get the Change War rolling?

Or suppose, in the far future, Terra's own spiders evolved intelligence and a cruel cannibal culture. They'd be able to keep their existence secret. I had no idea of who or what would be on Earth in Sevensee's day, and wouldn't it be perfect black hairy poisoned spider-mentality to spin webs secretly through the world of thought and all of space and time?

And Beau—wasn't there something real Snaky about him, the way he moved and all?

Spiders and Snakes. *Spinne und Schlange*, as Erich called them. S & S. But SS stood for the Nazi *Schutzstaffel*, the Black Shirts, and what if some of those cruel, crazy Jerries had discovered time travel and—I brought myself up with a jerk and asked myself, "Greta, how nuts can you get?"

From where he was on the floor, the front of the bar his sounding board, Doc shrieked up at Bruce like one of the damned from the pit, "Don't speak against the Spiders! Don't blaspheme! They can hear the Unborn whisper. Others whip only the skin, but they whip the naked brain and heart," and Erich called out, "That's enough, Bruce!"

But Bruce didn't spare him a look and said, "But whatever the Spiders are and no matter how much whip they use, it's plain as the telltale on the Maintainer that the Change War is not only going against them, but getting away from them. Dwell for a bit on the current flurry of stupid slugging and panicky anachronism, when we all know that anachronism is what gets the Change Winds out of control. This punch-drunk pounding on the Cretan-Dorian fracas as if it were the only battle going and the only way to work things. Whisking Constantine from Britain to the Bosporus by rocket, sending a pocket submarine back to sail with the Armada against Drake's woodensides—I'll wager you hadn't heard those! And now, to save Rome, an atomic bomb.

"Ye gods, they could have used Greek fire or even dynamite, but a fission weapon... I leave you to imagine what gaps and scars that will make in what's left of history—the smothering of Greece and the vanishment of Provence and the troubadours and the Papacy's Irish Captivity won't be in it!"

The cut on his cheek had opened again and was oozing a little, but he didn't pay any attention to it, and neither did we, as his lips thinned in irony and he said, "But I'm forgetting that this is a cosmic war and that the Spiders are conducting operations on billions, trillions of planets and inhabited gas clouds through millions of ages and that we're just one little world—one little solar system, Sevensee—and we can hardly expect our inscrutable masters, with all their pressing preoccupations and far-flung responsibilities, to be especially understanding or tender in their treatment of our pet books and centuries, our favorite prophets and periods, or unduly concerned about preserving any of the trifles that we just happen to hold dear.

"Perhaps there are some sentimentalists who would rather die forever than go on living in a world without the *Summa*, the Field Equations, *Process and Reality*, *Hamlet*, Matthew, Keats, and the *Odyssey*, but our masters are practical creatures, ministering to the needs of those rugged souls who want to go on living no matter what."

Erich's "Bruce, I'm telling you that's enough," was lost in the quickening flow of the New Boy's words. "I won't spend much time on the minor signs of our major crack-up—the canceling of leaves, the sharper shortages, the loss of the Express Room, the use of Recuperation Stations for ops and all the other frantic patchwork—last operation but one, we were saddled with three Soldiers from outside the Galaxy and, no fault of theirs, they were no earthly use. Such little things might happen at a bad spot in any war and are perhaps only local. But there's a big thing."

He paused again, to let us wonder, I guess. Maud must have worked her way over to me, for I felt her dry little hand on my arm and she whispered out of the side of her mouth, "What do we do now?"

"We listen," I told her the same way. I felt a little impatient with her need to be doing something about things.

She cocked a gold-dusted eyebrow at me and murmured, "You, too?"

I didn't get to ask her me, too, what? Crush on Bruce? Nuts!—because just then Bruce's voice took up again in the faraway range.

"Have you ever asked yourselves how many operations the fabric of history can stand before it's all stitches, whether too much Change won't one day wear out the past? And the present and the future, too, the whole bleeding business. Is the law of the Conservation of Reality any more than a thin hope given a long name, a prayer of theoreticians? Change Death is as certain as Heat Death, and far faster. Every operation leaves reality a bit cruder, a bit uglier, a bit more makeshift, and a whole lot less rich in those details and feelings that are our heritage, like the crude penciled sketch on canvas when you've stripped off the paint.

"If that goes on, won't the cosmos collapse into an outline of itself, then nothing? How much thinning can reality stand, having more and more Doublegangers cut out of it? And there's another thing about every operation—it wakes up the Zombies a little more, and as its Change Winds die, it leaves them a little more disturbed and nightmare-ridden and frazzled. Those of you who have been on operations in heavily worked-over temporal areas will know what I mean— that look they give you out of the sides of their eyes as if to say, 'You again? For Christ's sake, go away. We're the dead.

We're the ones who don't want to wake up, who don't want to be Demons and hate to be Ghosts. Stop torturing us.' "

I looked around at the Ghostgirls; I couldn't help it. They'd somehow got together on the control divan, facing us, their backs to the Maintainers. The Countess had dragged along the bottle of wine Erich had fetched her earlier and they were passing it back and forth. The Countess had a big rose splotch across the ruffled white lace of her blouse.

Bruce said, "There'll come a day when all the Zombies and all the Unborn wake up and go crazy together and figuratively come marching at us in their numberless hordes, saying, 'We've had enough.'"

But I didn't turn back to Bruce right away. Phryne's chiton had slipped off one shoulder and she and the Countess were sitting sagged forward, elbows on knees, legs spread—at least, as far as the Countess's hobble skirt would let her—and swayed toward each other a little. They were still surprisingly solid, although they hadn't had any personal attention for a half hour, and they were looking up over my head with half-shut eyes and they seemed, so help me, to be listening to what Bruce was saying and maybe hearing some of it.

"We make a careful distinction between Zombies and Unborn, between those troubled by our operations whose lifelines lie in the past and those whose lifelines lie in the future. But is there any distinction any longer? Can we tell the difference between the past and the future? Can we any longer locate the now, the real now of the cosmos? The Places have their own nows, the now of the Big Time we're on, but that's different and it's not made for real living.

"The Spiders tell us that the real now is somewhere in the last half of the 20th Century, which means that several of us here are also alive in the cosmos, have lifelines along which the now is traveling. But do you swallow that story quite so easily, Ilhilihis, Sevensee? How does it strike the servants of the Triple Goddess? The Spiders of Octavian Rome? The Demons of Good Queen Bess? The gentlemen Zombies of the Greater South? Do the Unborn man the starships, Maud?

"The Spiders also tell us that, although the fog of battle makes the now hard to pin down precisely, it will return with the unconditional surrender of the Snakes and the establishment of cosmic peace, and roll on as majestically toward the future as before, quickening the continuum with its passage. Do you really believe that? Or do you believe, as I do, that we've used up all the future as well as the past, wasted it in premature experience, and that we've had the real now smudged out of existence, stolen from us forever, the precious now of true growth, the child-moment in which all life lies, the moment like a newborn baby that is the only home for hope there is?"

He let that start to sink in, then took a couple of quick steps and went on, his voice rising over Erich's "Bruce, for the last time..." And seeming to pick up a note of hope from the very word he had used, "But although things look terrifyingly black, there remains a chance—the slimmest chance, but still a chance—of saving the cosmos from Change Death and restoring reality's richness and giving the Ghosts good sleep and perhaps even regaining the real now. We have the means right at hand. What if the power of time traveling were used not for war and destruction, but for healing, for the mutual enrichment of the ages, for quiet communication and growth, in brief, to bring a peace message—"

But my little commandant is quite an actor himself and knows a wee bit about the principles of scene-stealing, and he was not going to let Bruce drown him out as if he were just another extra playing a Voice from the Mob. He darted across our front, between us and the bar, took a running leap, and landed bang on the bloody box of bomb.

A bit later, Maud was silently showing me the white ring above her elbow where I'd grabbed her and Illy was teasing a clutch of his tentacles out of my other hand and squeaking reproachfully, "Greta girl, don't ever do that."

Erich was standing on the chest and I noticed that his boots carefully straddled the circle of skulls, and I should have known anyway you could hardly push them in the right order by jumping on them, and he was pointing at Bruce and saying, "—and that means mutiny, my young sir. *Um Gottes willen*, Bruce, listen to me and step down before you say anything worse. I'm older than you, Bruce. Mark's older. Trust in your *Kameraden*. Guide yourself by their knowledge."

He had got my attention, but I had much rather have him black my eye.

"You older than me?" Bruce was grinning. "When your twelve-years' advantage was spent in soaking up the wisdom of a race of sadistic dreamers gone paranoid, in a world whose thought-stream had already been muddied by one total war? Mark older than me? When all his ideas and loyalties are those of a wolf pack of unimaginative sluggers two thousand years younger than I am? Either of you older because you have more of the killing cynicism that is all the wisdom the Change World ever gives you? Don't make me laugh!

"I'm an Englishman, and I come from an epoch when total war was still a desecration and the flowers and buds of thoughts not yet whacked off or blighted. I'm a poet and poets are wiser than anyone because they're the only people who have the guts to think and feel at the same time. Right, Sid? When I talk to all of you about a peace message, I want you to think about it concretely in terms of using the Places to bring help across the mountains of time when help is really needed, not to bring help that's undeserved or knowledge that's premature or contaminating, sometimes not to bring anything at all, but just to check with infinite tenderness and concern that everything's safe and the glories of the universe unfolding as they were intended to—"

"Yes, you are a poet, Bruce," Erich broke in. "You can tootle soulfully on the flute and make us drip tears. You can let out the stops on the big organ pipes and make us tremble as if at Jehovah's footsteps. For the last twenty minutes, you have been giving us some very *charmante* poetry. But what are you? An Entertainer? Or are you a Soldier?"

Right then—I don't know what it was, maybe Sid clearing his throat—I could sense our feelings beginning to turn against Bruce. I got the strangest feeling of reality clamping down and bright colors going dull and dreams vanishing. Yet it was only then I also realized how much Bruce had moved us, maybe some of us to the verge of mutiny, even. I was mad at Erich for what he was doing, but I couldn't help admiring his cockiness.

I was still under the spell of Bruce's words and the more-than-words behind them, but then Erich would shift around a bit and one of his heels would kick near the death's-head pushbuttons and I wanted to stamp with spike heels on every death's-head button on his uniform. I didn't know exactly what I felt yet.

"Yes, I'm a Soldier," Bruce told him, "and I hope you won't ever have to worry about my courage, because it's going to take more courage than any operation we've ever planned, ever dreamed of, to carry the peace message to the other Places and to the wound-spots of the cosmos. Perhaps it will be a fast wicket and we'll be bowled down before we score a single run, but who cares? We may at least see our real masters when they come to smash us, and for me that will be a deep satisfaction. And we may do some smashing of our own."

"So you're a Soldier," Erich said, his smile showing his teeth. "Bruce, I'll admit that the half-dozen operations you've been on were rougher than anything I drew in my first hundred sleeps. For that, I am all honest sympathy. But that you should let them get you into such a state that love and a girl can turn you upside down and start you babbling about peace messages—"

"Yes, by God, love and a girl have changed me!" Bruce shouted at him, and I looked around at Lili and I remembered Dave saying, "I'm going to Spain," and I wondered if anything would ever again make my face flame like that. "Or, rather, they've made me stand up for what I've believed in all along. They've made me—"

"*Wunderbar,*" Erich called and began to do a little sissy dance on the bomb that set my teeth on edge. He bent his wrists and elbows at arty angles and stuck out a hip and ducked his head simperingly and blinked his eyes very fast. "Will you invite me to the wedding, Bruce? You'll have to get another best man, but I will be the flower girl and throw pretty little posies to all the distinguished guests. Here, Mark. Catch, Kaby. One for you, Greta. *Danke schön. Ach, zwei Herzen in dreivierteltakt...ta-ta...ta-ta...ta-ta-ta-ta-ta...*"

"What the hell do you think a woman is?" Bruce raged. "Something to mess around with in your spare time?"

Erich kept on humming "Two Hearts in Waltz Time" and jigging around to it, damn him—but he slipped in a nod to Bruce and a "Precisely." So I knew where I stood, but it was no news to me.

"Very well," Bruce said, "let's leave this Brown Shirt *maricón* to amuse himself and get down to business. I made all of you a proposal and I don't have to tell you how serious it is or how serious Lili and I are about it. We not only must infiltrate and subvert other Places, which luckily for us are made for infiltration, we also must make contact with the Snakes and establish working relationships with their Demons at our level as one of our first steps."

That stopped Erich's jig and got enough of a gasp from some of us to make it seem to come from practically everybody. Erich used it to work a change of pace.

"Bruce! We've let you carry this foolery further than we should. You seem to have the idea that because anything goes in the Place—dueling, drunkenness, *und so weiter*—you can say what you have and it will all be forgotten with the hangover. Not so. It is true that among such a set of monsters and free spirits as ourselves, and working as secret agents to boot, there cannot be the obvious military discipline that would obtain in a Terran army.

"But let me tell you, Bruce, let me grind it home into you—Sid and Kaby and Mark will bear me out in this, as officers of equivalent rank—that the Spider line of command stretches into and through this Place just as surely as the word of *der Führer* rules Chicago. And as I shouldn't have to emphasize to you, Bruce, the Spiders have punishments that would make my countrymen in Belsen and Buchenwald— well, pale a little. So while there is still a shadow of justification for our interpreting your remarks as utterly tasteless clowning—"

"Babble on," Bruce said, giving him a loose downward wave of his hand without looking. "I made you people a proposal." He paused. "How do you stand, Sidney Lessingham?"

Then I felt my legs getting weak, because Sid didn't answer right away. The old boy swallowed and started to look around at the rest of us. Then the feeling of reality clamping down got something awful, because he didn't look around, but straightened his back a little. Just then, Mark cut in fast.

"It grieves me, Bruce, but I think you are possessed. Erich, he must be confined."

Kaby nodded, almost absently. "Confine or kill the coward, whichever is easier, whip the woman, and let's get on to the Egyptian battle."

"Indeed, yes," Mark said. "I died in it. But now perhaps no longer."

Kaby said to him, "I like you, Roman."

Bruce was smiling, barely, and his eyes were moving and fixing. "You, Ilhilihis?"

Illy's squeak box had never sounded mechanical to me before, but it did as he answered, "I'm a lot deeper into borrowed time than the rest of you, tra-la-la, but Papa still loves living. Include me very much out, Brucie."

"Miss Davies?"

Beside me, Maud said flatly, "Do you think I'm a fool?" Beyond her, I saw Lili and I thought, "My God, I might look as proud if I were in her shoes, but I sure as hell wouldn't look as confident."

Bruce's eyes hadn't quite come to Beau when the gambler spoke up. "I have no cause to like you, sir, rather the opposite. But this Place has come to bore me more than Boston and I have always found it difficult to resist a long shot. A very long one, I fear. I am with you, sir."

There was a pain in my chest and a roaring in my ears and through it I heard Sevensee grunting, "Sicka these lousy Spiders. Deal me in."

And then Doc reared up in front of the bar and he'd lost his hat and his hair was wild and he grabbed an empty fifth by the neck and broke the bottom of it all jagged against the bar and he waved it and screeched, "*Ubivaytye Pauki—i Nyemetzi!*"

And right behind his words, Beau sang out fast the English of it, "Kill the Spiders—and the Germans!"

And Doc didn't collapse then, though I could see he was hanging onto the bar tight with his other hand, and the Place got stiller, inside and out, than I've ever known it, and Bruce's eyes were finally moving back toward Sid.

But the eyes stopped short of Sid and I heard Bruce say, "Miss Forzane?" and I thought, "That's funny," and I started to look around at the Countess, and felt all the eyes and I realized, "Hey, that's me! But this can't happen to me. To the others, yes, but not to me. I just work here. Not to Greta, no, no, no!"

But it had, and the eyes didn't let go, and the silence and the feeling of reality were Godawful, and I said to myself, "Greta, you've got to say something, if only a suitable four-letter word," and then suddenly I knew what the silence was like. It was like that of a big city if there were some way of shutting off all the noise in one second. It was like Erich's singing when the piano had deserted him. It was as if the Change Winds should ever die completely…and I knew beforehand what had happened when I turned my back on them all.

The Ghostgirls were gone. The Major Maintainer hadn't merely been switched to Introvert. It was gone, too.

CHAPTER NINE
A Locked Room

"We examined the moss between the bricks, and found it undisturbed."

"You looked among D——'s papers, of course, and into the books of the library?"

"Certainly; we opened every package and parcel; we not only opened every book, but we turned over every leaf in each volume…"

—Poe

Three hours later, Sid and I plumped down on the couch nearest the kitchen, though too tired to want to eat for a while yet. A tighter search than I could ever have cooked up had shown that the Maintainer was not in the Place.

Of course it had to be in the Place, as we kept telling each other for the first two hours. It had to be, if circumstances and the theories we lived by in the Change World meant anything. A Maintainer is what maintains a Place. The Minor Maintainer takes care of oxygen, temperature, humidity, gravity, and other little life-cycle and matter-cycle things generally, but it's the Major Maintainer that keeps the walls from buckling and the ceiling from falling in. It is little, but oh my, it does so much.

It doesn't work by wires or radio or anything complicated like that. It just hooks into local space-time.

I have been told that its inside working part is made up of vastly tough, vastly hard giant molecules, each one of which is practically a vest-pocket cosmos in itself. Outside, it looks like a portable radio with a few more dials and some telltales and switches and plug-ins for earphones and a lot of other sensory thingumajigs.

But the Maintainer was gone and the Void hadn't closed in, yet. By this time, I was so fagged, I didn't care much whether it did or not.

One thing for sure, the Maintainer had been switched to Introvert before it was spirited away or else its disappearance automatically produced Introversion, take your choice, because we sure were Introverted—real nasty martinet-schoolmaster grip of reality on my thoughts that I knew, without trying, liquor wouldn't soften, not a breath of Change Wind, absolutely stifling, and the gray of the Void seeming so much inside my head that I think I got a glimmering of what the science boys mean when they explain to me that the Place is a kind of interweaving of the material and the mental—a Giant Monad, one of them called it.

Anyway, I said to myself, "Greta, if this is Introversion, I want no part of it. It is not nice to be cut adrift from the cosmos and know it. A lifeboat in the middle of the Pacific and a starship between galaxies are not in it for loneliness."

I asked myself why the Spiders had ever equipped Maintainers with Introversion switches anyway, when we couldn't drill with them and weren't supposed to use them except in an emergency so tight that it was either Introvert or surrender to the Snakes, and for the first time the obvious explanation came to me:

Introversion must be the same as scuttling, its main purpose to withhold secrets and materiel from the enemy. It put a place into a situation from which even the Spider high command couldn't rescue it, and there was nothing left but to sink down, down (out? up?), down into the Void.

If that was the case, our chances of getting back were about those of my being a kid again playing in the Dunes on the Small Time.

I edged a little closer to Sid and sort of squunched under his shoulder and rubbed my cheek against the smudged, gold-worked gray velvet. He looked down and I said, "A long way to Lynn Regis, eh, Siddy?"

"Sweetling, thou spokest a mouthful," he said. He knows very well what he is doing when he mixes his language that way, the wicked old darling.

"Siddy," I said, "why this gold-work? It'd be a lot smoother without it."

"Marry, men must prick themselves out and, 'faith I know not, but it helps if there's metal in it."

"And girls get scratched." I took a little sniff. "But don't put this doublet through the cleaner yet. Until we get out of the woods, I want as much you around as possible."

"Marry, and why should I?" he asked blankly, and I think he wasn't fooling me. The last thing time travelers find out is how they do or don't smell. Then his face clouded and he looked as though he wanted to squunch under my shoulder. "But 'faith, sweetling, your forest has a few more trees than Sherwood."

"Thou saidst it," I agreed, and wondered about the look. He oughtn't to be interested in my girlishness now. I knew I was a mess, but he had stuck pretty close to me during the hunt and you never can tell. Then I remembered that he was the other one who hadn't declared himself when Bruce was putting it to us, and it probably troubled his male vanity. Not me, though—I was still grateful to the Maintainer for getting me out of that spot, whatever other it had got us all into. It seemed ages ago.

We'd all jumped to the conclusion that the two Ghostgirls had run away with the Maintainer, I don't know where or why, but it looked so much that way. Maud had started yipping about how she'd never trusted Ghosts and always known that some day they'd start doing things on their own, and Kaby had got it firmly fixed in her head, right between the horns, that Phryne, being a Greek, was the ringleader and was going to wreak havoc on us all.

But when we were checking Stores the first time, I had noticed that the Ghostgirl envelopes looked flat. Ectoplasm doesn't take up much space when it's folded, but I had opened one anyway, then another, and then called for help.

Every last envelope was empty. We had lost over a thousand Ghostgirls, Sid's whole stock.

Well, at least it proved what none of us had ever seen or heard of being demonstrated: that there is a spooky link—a sort of Change Wind contact—between a Ghost and its lifeline; and when that umbilicus, I've heard it called, is cut, the part away from the lifeline dies.

Interesting, but what had bothered me was whether we Demons were going to evaporate too, because we are as much

Doublegangers as the Ghosts and our apron strings had been cut just as surely. We're more solid, of course, but that would only mean we'd take a little longer. Very logical.

I remember I had looked up at Lili and Maud—us girls had been checking the envelopes; it's one of the proprieties we frequently maintain and anyway, if men check them, they're apt to trot out that old wheeze about "instant women" which I'm sick to death of hearing, thank you.

Anyway, I had looked up and said, "It's been nice knowing you," and Lili had said, "Twenty-three, skiddoo," and Maud had said, "Here goes nothing," and we had shook hands all around.

We figured that Phryne and the Countess had faded at the same time as the other Ghostgirls, but an idea had been nibbling at me and I said, "Siddy, do you suppose it's just barely possible that, while we were all looking at Bruce, those two Ghostgirls would have been able to work the Maintainer and get a Door and lam out of here with the thing?"

"Thou speakst my thoughts, sweetling. All weighs against it: Imprimis, 'tis well known that Ghosts cannot lay plots or act on them. Secundo, the time forbade getting a Door. Tercio—and here's the real meat of it—the Place folds without the Maintainer. Quadro, 'twere folly to depend on not one of—how many of us? ten, elf—not looking around in all the time it would have taken them—"

"I looked around once, Siddy. They were drinking and they had got to the control divan under their own power. Now when was that? Oh, yes, when Bruce was talking about Zombies."

"Yes, sweetling. And as I was about to cap my argument with quinquo when you 'gan prattle, I could have sworn none could touch the Maintainer, much less work it and purloin it, without my certain knowledge. Yet…"

"Eftsoons yet," I seconded him.

Somebody must have got a door and walked out with the thing. It certainly wasn't in the Place. The hunt had been a lulu. Something the size of a portable typewriter is not easy to hide and we had been inside everything from Beau's piano to the renewer link of the Refresher.

We had even fluoroscoped everybody, though it had made Illy writhe like a box of worms, as he'd warned us; he said it tickled terribly and I insisted on smoothing his fur for five minutes afterward, although he was a little standoffish toward me.

Some areas, like the bar, kitchen and Stores, took a long while, but we were thorough. Kaby helped Doc check Surgery: since she last made the Place, she has been stationed in a Field Hospital (it turns out the Spiders actually are mounting operations from them) and learned a few nice new wrinkles.

However, Doc put in some honest work on his own, though, of course, every check was observed by at least three people, not including Bruce or Lili. When the Maintainer vanished, Doc had pulled out of his glassy-eyed drunk in a way that would have surprised me if I hadn't seen it happen to him before, but when we finished Surgery and got on to the Art Gallery, he had started to putter and I noticed him hold out his coat and duck his head and whip out a flask and take a swig and by now he was well on his way toward another peak.

The Art Gallery had taken time too, because there's such a jumble of strange stuff, and it broke my heart but Kaby took her ax and split a beautiful blue woodcarving of a Venusian medusa because, although there wasn't a mark in the paw-polished surface, she claimed it was just big enough. Doc cried a little and we left him fitting the pieces together and mooning over the other stuff.

After we'd finished everything else, Mark had insisted on tackling the floor. Beau and Sid both tried to explain to him how this is a one-sided Place, that there is nothing, but nothing, under the floor; it just gets a lot harder than the diamonds crusting it as soon as you get a quarter inch down— that being the solid equivalent of the Void. But Mark was knuckle-headed (like all Romans, Sid assured me on the q.t.) and broke four diamond-plus drills before he was satisfied.

Except for some trick hiding places, that left the Void, and things don't vanish if you throw them at the Void—they half melt and freeze forever unless you can fish them out. Back of the Refresher, at about eye-level, are three Venusian coconuts that a Hittite strongman threw there during a major brawl. I try not to look at them because they are so much like witch heads they give me the woolies. The parts of the Place right up against the Void have strange spatial properties which one of the gadgets in Surgery makes use of in a way that gives me the worse woolies, but that's beside the point.

During the hunt, Kaby and Erich had used their Callers as direction finders to point out the Maintainer, just as they're used in the cosmos to locate the Door—and sometimes in the Big Places, people tell me. But the Callers only went wild— like a compass needle whirling around without stopping—and nobody knew what that meant.

The trick hiding places were the Minor Maintainer, a cute idea, but it is no bigger than the Major and has its own mysterious insides and had obviously kept on doing its own work, so that was out for several reasons, and the bomb chest, though it seemed impossible for anyone to have opened it, granting they knew the secret of its lock, even before Erich jumped on it and put it in the limelight double. But when you've ruled out everything else, the word impossible changes meaning.

Since time travel is our business, a person might think of all sorts of tricks for sending the Maintainer into the past or future, permanently or temporarily. But the Place is strictly on the Big Time and everybody that should know tells me that time traveling *through* the Big Time is out. It's this way: the Big Time is a train, and the Little Time is the countryside and we're on the train, unless we go out a Door, and as Gertie Stein might put it, you can't time travel through the time you time travel in when you time travel.

I'd also played around with the idea of some fantastically obvious hiding place, maybe something that several people could pass back and forth between them, which would mean a conspiracy, and, of course, if you assume a big enough conspiracy, you can explain anything, including the cosmos itself. Still, I'd got a sort of shell-game idea about the Soldiers' three big black shakos and I hadn't been satisfied until I'd got the three together and looked in them all at the same time.

"Wake up, Greta, and take something. I can't stand here forever." Maud had brought us a tray of hearty snacks from then and yon, and I must say they were tempting; she whips up a mean hors d'oeuvre.

I looked them over and said, "Siddy, I want a hot dog."

"And I want a venison pasty! Out upon you, you finical jill, you o'erscrupulous jade, you whimsic and tyrannous poppet!"

I grabbed a handful and snuggled back against him.

"Go on, call me some more, Siddy," I told him. "Real juicy ones."

CHAPTER TEN
Motives and Opportunities

*My thought, whose murder yet is but fantastical, Shakes so my single
state of man that function Is smother'd in surmise, and nothing is But
what is not.*
—*Macbeth*

My big bad waif from King's Lynn had set the tray on his
knees and started to wolf the food down. The others were
finishing up. Erich, Mark and Kaby were having a quietly
furious argument I couldn't overhear at the end of the bar
nearest the bronze chest, and Illy was draped over the piano
like a real octopus, listening in.

Beau and Sevensee were pacing up and down near the
control divan and throwing each other a word now and then.
Beyond them, Bruce and Lili were sitting on the opposite
couch from us, talking earnestly about something. Maud had
sat down at the other end of the bar and was knitting—it's
one of the habits like chess and quiet drinking, or learning to
talk by squeak box, that we pick up to pass the time in the
Place in the long stretches between parties. Doc was fiddling
around the Gallery, picking things up and setting them down,
still managing to stay on his feet at any rate.

Lili and Bruce stood up, still gabbing intensely at each
other, and Illy began to pick out with one tentacle a little tune
in the high keys that didn't sound like anything on God's
earth. "Where do they get all the energy?" I wondered.

As soon as I asked myself that, I knew the answer and I
began to feel the same way myself. It wasn't energy; it was
nerves, pure and simple.

Change is like a drug, I realized—you get used to the facts never staying the same, and one picture of the past and future dissolving into another maybe not very different but still different, and your mind being constantly goosed by strange moods and notions, like nightclub lights of shifting color with weird shadows between shining right on your brain.

The endless swaying and jogging is restful, like riding on a train.

You soon get to like the movement and to need it without knowing, and when it suddenly stops and you're just you and the facts you think from and feel from are exactly the same when you go back to them—boy, that's rough, as I found out now.

The instant we got Introverted, everything that ordinarily leaks into the Place, wake or sleep, had stopped coming, and we were nothing but ourselves and what we meant to each other and what we could make of that, an awfully lonely, scratchy situation.

I decided I felt like I'd been dropped into a swimming pool full of cement and held under until it hardened.

I could understand the others bouncing around a bit. It was a wonder they didn't hit the Void. Maud seemed to be standing it the best; maybe she'd got a little preparation from the long watches between stars; and then she is older than all of us, even Sid, though with a small "o" in "older."

The restless work of the search for the Maintainer had masked the feeling, but now it was beginning to come full force. Before the search, Bruce's speech and Erich's interruptions had done a passable masking job too. I tried to remember when I'd first got the feeling and decided it was after Erich had jumped on the bomb, about the time he mentioned poetry. Though I couldn't be sure. Maybe the Maintainer had been Introverted even earlier, when I'd turned to look at the Ghostgirls. I wouldn't have known. Nuts!

Believe me, I could feel that hardened cement on every inch of me. I remembered Bruce's beautiful picture of a universe without Big Change and decided it was about the worst idea going. I went on eating, though I wasn't so sure now it was a good idea to keep myself strong.

"Does the Maintainer have an Introversion telltale? Siddy!"

"'Sdeath, chit, and you love me, speak lower. Of a sudden, I feel not well, as if I'd drunk a butt of Rhenish and slept inside it. Marry yes, blue. In short flashes, saith the manual. Why ask'st thou?"

"No reason. God, Siddy, what I'd give for a breath of Change Wind."

"Thou can'st say that eftsoons," he groaned. I must have looked pretty miserable myself, for he put his arm around my shoulders and whispered gruffly, "Comfort thyself, sweetling, that while we suffer thus sorely, we yet cannot die the Change Death."

"What's that?" I asked him.

I didn't want to bounce around like the others. I had a suspicion I'd carry it too far. So, to keep myself from going batty, I started to rework the business of who had done what to the Maintainer.

During the hunt, there had been some pretty wild suggestions tossed around as to its disappearance or at least its Introversion: a feat of Snake science amounting to sorcery; the Spider high command bunkering the Places from above, perhaps in reaction to the loss of the Express Room, in such a hurry that they hadn't even time to transmit warnings; the hand of the Late Cosmicians, those mysterious hypothetical beings who are supposed to have successfully resisted the extension of the Change War into the future much beyond Sevensee's epoch—unless the Late Cosmicians are the ones fighting the Change War.

One thing these suggestions had steered very clear of was naming any one of us as a suspect, whether acting as Snake spy, Spider political police, agent of—who knows, after Bruce?—a secret Change World Committee of Public Safety or Spider revolutionary underground, or strictly on our own. Just as no one had piped a word, since the Maintainer had been palmed, about the split between Erich's and Bruce's factions.

Good group thinking probably, to sink differences in the emergency, but that didn't apply to what I did with my own thoughts.

Who wanted to escape so bad they'd Introvert the Place, cutting off all possible contact and communication either way with the cosmos and running the very big risk of not getting back to the cosmos at all?

Leaving out what had happened since Bruce had arrived and stirred things up, Doc seemed to me to have the strongest motive. He knew that Sid couldn't keep covering up for him forever and that Spider punishments for derelictions of duty are not just the clink of a firing squad, as Erich had reminded us. But Doc had been flat on the floor in front of the bar from the time Bruce had jumped on top of it, though I certainly hadn't had my eye on him every second.

Beau? Beau had said he was bored with the Place at a time when what he said counted, so he'd hardly lock himself in it maybe forever, not to mention locking Bruce in with himself and the babe he had a yen for.

Sid loves reality, Changing or not, and every least thing in it, people especially, more than any man or woman I've ever known—he's like a big-eyed baby who wants to grab every object and put it in his mouth—and it was hard to imagine him ever cutting himself off from the cosmos.

Maud, Kaby, Mark and the two ETs? None of them had any motive I knew of, though Sevensee's being from the very far future did tie in with that idea about the Late Cosmicians, and there did seem to be something developing between the Cretan and the Roman that could make them want to be Introverted together.

"Stick to the facts, Greta," I reminded myself with a private groan.

That left Erich, Bruce, Lili and myself.

Erich, I thought—now we're getting somewhere. The little commandant has the nervous system of a coyote and the courage of a crazy tomcat, and if he thought it would help him settle his battle with Bruce better to be locked in with him, he'd do it in a second.

But even before Erich had danced on the bomb, he'd been heckling Bruce from the crowd. Still, there would have been time between heckles for him to step quietly back from us, Introvert the Maintainer and...well, that was nine-tenths of the problem.

If I was the guilty party, I was nuts and that was the best explanation of all. Gr-r-r!

Bruce's motives seemed so obvious, especially the mortal (or was it immortal?) danger he'd put himself in by inciting mutiny, that it seemed a shame he'd been in full view on the bar so long. Surely, if the Maintainer had been Introverted before he jumped on the bar, we'd all have noticed the flashing blue telltale. For that matter, I'd have noticed it when I looked back at the Ghostgirls—if it worked as Sid claimed, and he said he had never seen it in operation, just read in the manual—oh, 'sdeath!

But Bruce didn't need opportunity, as I'm sure all the males in the Place would have told me right off, because he had Lili to pull the job for him and she had as much opportunity as any of the rest of us. Myself, I have large reservations to this woman-putty-in-the-hands-of-the-man-she-loves-madly theory, but I had to admit there was something to be said for it in this case, and it had seemed quite natural to me when the rest of us had decided, by unspoken agreement, that neither Lili's nor Bruce's checks counted when we were hunting for the Maintainer.

That took care of all of us and left only the mysterious stranger, intruding somehow through a Door (how'd he get it without using our Maintainer?) or from an unimaginable hiding place or straight out of the Void itself. I know that last is impossible—nothing can step out of nothing—but if anything ever looked like it was specially built for something not at all nice to come looming out of, it's the Void—misty, foggily churning, slimy gray...

"Wait a second," I told myself, "and hang onto this, Greta. It should have smacked you in the face at the start."

Whatever came out of the Void, or, more to the point, whoever slipped back from our crowd to the Maintainer, Bruce would have seen them. He was looking at the Maintainer past our heads the whole time, and whatever happened to it, he saw it.

Erich wouldn't have, even after he was on the bomb, because he'd been stagewise enough to face Bruce most of the time to build up his role as tribune of the people.

But Bruce would have—unless he got so caught up in what he was saying...

No, kid, a Demon is always an actor, no matter how much he believes in what he's saying, and there never was an actor yet who wouldn't instantly notice a member of the audience starting to walk out on his big scene.

So Bruce knew, which made him a better actor than I'd have been willing to grant, since it didn't look as if anyone else had thought of what had just occurred to me, or they'd have gone over and put it to him.

Not me, though—I don't work that way. Besides, I didn't feel up to it—Nervy Anna enfold me, I felt like pure hell.

"Maybe," I told myself encouragingly, "the Place is Hell," but added, "Be your age, Greta—be a real rootless, ruleless, ruthless twenty-nine."

CHAPTER ELEVEN
The Western Front, 1917

The barrage roars and lifts. Then, clumsily bowed With bombs and guns and shovels and battle gear, Men jostle and climb to meet the bristling fire. Lines of gray, muttering faces, masked with fear, They leave their trenches, going over the top, While time ticks blank and busy on their wrists
—Sassoon

"Please don't, Lili."

"I shall, my love."

"Sweetling, wake up! Hast the shakes?"

I opened my eyes a little and lied to Siddy with a smile and locked my hands together tight and watched Bruce and Lili quarrel nobly near the control divan and wished I had a great love to blur my misery and provide me with a passable substitute for Change Winds.

Lili won the argument, judging from the way she threw her head back and stepped away from Bruce's arms while giving him a proud, tender smile. He walked off a few steps; praise be, he didn't shrug his shoulders at us like an old husband, though his nerves were showing and he didn't seem to be standing Introversion well at all, as who of us were?

Lili rested a hand on the head of the control divan and pressed her lips together and looked around at us, mostly with her eyes. She'd wound a gray silk bandeau around her bangs. Her short gray silk dress without a waistline made her look, not so much like a flapper, though she looked like that all right, as like a little girl, except the neckline was scooped low enough to show she wasn't.

Her gaze hesitated and then stopped at me and I got a sunk feeling of what was coming, because women are always picking on me for an audience. Besides, Sid and I were the centrist party of two in our fresh-out-of-the-shell Place politics.

She took a deep breath and stuck out her chin and said in a voice that was even a little higher and Britisher than she usually uses, "We girls have often cried, 'Shut the Door!' But now the Door is jolly well shut for keeps!"

I knew I'd guessed right and I felt crawly with embarrassment, because I know about this love business of thinking you're the other person and trying to live their life—and grab their glory, though you don't know that—and carry their message for them, and how it can foul things up. Still, I couldn't help admitting what she said wasn't too bad a start—unpleasantly apt to be true, at any rate.

"My fiance believes we may yet be able to open the Door. I do not. He thinks it is a bit premature to discuss the peculiar pickle in which we all find ourselves. I do not."

There was a rasp of laughter from the bar. The militarists were reacting. Erich stepped out, looking very happy. "So now we have to listen to women making speeches," he called. "What is this Place, anyhow? Sidney Lessingham's Saturday Evening Sewing Circle?"

Beau and Sevensee, who'd stopped their pacing halfway between the bar and the control divan, turned toward Erich, and Sevensee looked a little burlier, a little more like half a horse, than satyrs in mythology book illustrations. He stamped—medium hard, I'd say—and said, "Ahh, go flya kite." I'd found out he'd learned English from a Demon who'd been a longshoreman with syndicalist-anarchist sympathies. Erich shut up for a moment and stood there grinning, his hands on his hips.

Lili nodded to the satyr and cleared her throat, looking scared. But she didn't speak; I could see she was thinking and feeling something, and her face got ugly and haggard, as if she were in a Change Wind that hadn't reached me yet, and her mouth went into a snarl to fight tears, but some spurted out, and when she did speak her voice was an octave lower and it wasn't just London talking but New York too.

"I don't know how Resurrection felt to you people, because I'm new and I loathe asking questions, but to me it was pure torture and I wished only I'd had the courage to tell Suzaku, 'I wish to remain a Zombie, if you don't mind. I'd rather the nightmares.' But I accepted Resurrection because I've been taught to be polite and because there is the Demon in me I don't understand that always wishes to live, and I found that I still felt like a Zombie, although I could flit about, and that I still had the nightmares, except they'd grown a deal vivider.

"I was a young girl again, seventeen, and I suppose every woman wishes to be seventeen, but I wasn't seventeen inside my head—I was a woman who had died of Bright's disease in New York in 1929 and also, because a Big Change blew my lifeline into a new drift, a woman who had died of the same disease in Nazi-occupied London in 1955, but rather more slowly because, as you can fancy, the liquor was in far shorter supply. I had to live with both those sets of memories and the Change World didn't blot them out any more than I'm told it does those of any Demon, and it didn't even push them into the background as I'd hoped it would.

"When some Change Fellow would say to me, 'Hallo, beautiful, how about a smile?' or 'That's a posh frock, kiddo,' I'd be back at Bellevue looking down at my swollen figure and the light getting like spokes of ice, or in that dreadful gin-steeped Stepney bedroom with Phyllis coughing herself to death beside me, or at best, for a moment, a little girl in Glamorgan looking at the Roman road and wondering about the wonderful life that lay ahead."

I looked at Erich, remembering he had a long nasty future back in the cosmos himself, and at any rate he wasn't smiling, and I thought maybe he's getting a little humility, knowing someone else has two of those futures, but I doubted it.

"Because, you see," Lili kept forcing it out, "all my three lives I'd been a girl who fell in love with a great young poet she'd never met, the voice of the new youth and all youth, and she'd told her first big lie to get in the Red Cross and across to France to be nearer him, and it was all danger and dark magics and a knight in armor, and she pictured how she'd find him wounded but not seriously, with a little bandage around his head, and she'd light a fag for him and smile lightly, never letting him guess what she felt, but only being her best self and watching to see if that made something happen to him...

"And then the Boche machine guns cut him down at Passchendaele and there couldn't ever have been bandages big enough and the girl stayed seventeen inside and messed about and tried to be wicked, though she wasn't very good at that, and to drink, and she had a bit more talent there, though drinking yourself to death is not nearly as easy as it sounds, even with a kidney weakness to help. But she turned the trick.

"Then a cock crows. She wakes with a tearing start from the gray dreams of death that fill her lifeline. It's cold daybreak. There's the smell of a French farm. She feels her ankles and they're not at all like huge rubber boots filled with water. They're not swollen the least bit. They're young legs.

"There's a little window and the tops of a row of trees that may be poplars when there's more light, and what there is shows cots like her own and heads under blankets, and hanging uniforms make large shadows and a girl is snoring.

There's a very distant rumble and it moves the window a bit. Then she remembers they're Red Cross girls many, many kilometers from Passchendaele and that Bruce Marchant is going to die at dawn today.

"In a few more minutes, he's going over the top where there's a crop-headed machine-gunner in field gray already looking down the sights and swinging the gun a bit. But she isn't going to die today. She's going to die in 1929 and 1955.

"And just as she's going mad, there's a creaking and out of the shadows tiptoes a Jap with a woman's hairdo and the whitest face and the blackest eyebrows. He's wearing a rose robe and a black sash which belts to his sides two samurai swords, but in his right hand he has a strange silver pistol. And he smiles at her as if they were brother and sister and lovers at the same time and he says, '*Voulez-vous vivre, mademoiselle?*' and she stares and he bobs his head and says, 'Missy wish live, yes, no?' "

Sid's paw closed quietly around my shaking hands. It always gets me to hear about anyone's Resurrection, and although mine was crazier, it also had the Krauts in it. I hoped she wouldn't go through the rest of the formula and she didn't.

"Five minutes later, he's gone down a stairs more like a ladder to wait below and she's dressing in a rush. Her clothes resist a little, as if they were lightly gummed to the hook and the stained wall, and she hates to touch them. It's getting lighter and her cot looks as if someone were still sleeping there, although it's empty, and she couldn't bring herself to put her hand on the place if her new life depended on it.

"She climbs down and her long skirt doesn't bother her because she knows how to swing it. Suzaku conducts her past a sentry who doesn't see them and a puffy-faced farmer in a smock coughing and spitting the night out of his throat. They cross the farmyard and it's filled with rose light and she sees the sun is up and she knows that Bruce Marchant has just bled to death.

"There's an empty open touring car chugging loudly, waiting for someone; it has huge muddy wheels with wooden spokes and a brass radiator that says 'Simplex.' But Suzaku leads her past it to a dunghill and bows apologetically and she steps through a Door."

I heard Erich say to the others at the bar, "How touching! Now shall I tell everyone about my operation?" But he didn't get much of a laugh.

"That's how Lilian Foster came into the Change World with its steel-engraved nightmares and its deadly pace and deadlier lassitudes. I was more alive than I ever had been before, but it was the kind of life a corpse might get from unending electrical shocks and I couldn't summon any purpose or hope and Bruce Marchant seemed farther away than ever.

"Then, not six hours ago, a Soldier in a black uniform came through the Door and I thought, 'It can't be, but it does look like his photographs,' and then I thought I heard someone say the name Bruce, and then he shouted as if to all the world that he was Bruce Marchant, and I knew there was a Resurrection beyond Resurrection, a true resurrection. Oh, Bruce—"

She looked at him and he was crying and smiling and all the young beauty flooded back into her face, and I thought, "It has to be Change Winds, but it can't be. Face it without slobbering, Greta—there's something that works bigger miracles than Change."

And she went on, "And then the Change Winds died when the Snakes vaporized the Maintainer or the Ghostgirls Introverted it and all three of them vanished so swiftly and silently that even Bruce didn't notice—those are the best explanations I can summon and I fancy one of them is true.

At all events, the Change Winds died and my past and even my futures became something I could bear lightly, because I have someone to bear them with me, and because at last I have a true future stretching out ahead of me, an unknown future which I shall create by living. Oh, don't you see that all of us have it now, this big opportunity?"

"*Hussa* for Sidney's suffragettes and the W.C.T.U.!" Erich cheered. "Beau, will you play us a medley of 'Hearts and Flowers' and 'Onward, Christian Soldiers'? I'm deeply moved, Lili. Where do the rest of us queue up for the Great Love Affair of the Century?"

CHAPTER TWELVE
A Big Opportunity

Now is a bearable burden. What buckles the back is the added weight of the past's mistakes and the future's fears.

I had to learn to close the front door to tomorrow and the back door to yesterday and settle down to here and now.

—Anonymous

Nobody laughed at Erich's screwball sarcasms and still I thought, "Yes, perish his hysterical little gray head, but he's half right—Lili's got the big thing now and she wants to serve it up to the rest of us on a platter, only love doesn't cook and cut that way."

Those weren't bad ideas she had about the Maintainer, though, especially the one about the Ghostgirls doing the Introverting—it would explain why there couldn't be Introversion drill, the manual stuff about blue flashes being window-dressing, and something disappearing without movement or transition is the sort of thing that might not catch the attention—and I guess they gave the others something to think about too, for there wasn't any follow-up to Erich's frantic sniping.

But I honestly didn't see where there was this big opportunity being stuck away in a gray sack in the Void and I began to wonder and I got the strangest feeling and I said to myself, "Hang onto your hat, Greta. It's hope."

"The dreadful thing about being a Demon is that you have all time to range through," Lili was saying with a smile. "You can never shut the back door to yesterday or the front door to tomorrow and simply live in the present. But now that's been done for us: the Door is shut, we need never again rehash the past or the future. The Spiders and Snakes can never find us, for who ever heard of a Place that was truly lost being rescued? And as those in the know have told me, Introversion is the end as far as those outside are concerned. So we're safe from the Spiders and Snakes, we need never be slaves or enemies again, and we have a Place in which to live our new lives, the Place prepared for us from the beginning."

She paused. "Surely you understand what I mean? Sidney and Beauregard and Dr. Pyeshkov are the ones who explained it to me. The Place is a balanced aquarium, just like the cosmos. No one knows how many ages of Big Time it has been in use, without a bit of new material being brought in— only luxuries and people—and not a bit of waste cast off. No one knows how many more ages it may not sustain life. I never heard of Minor Maintainers wearing out. We have all the future, all the security, anyone can hope for. We have a Place to live together."

You know, she was dead right and I realized that all the time I'd had the conviction in the back of my mind that we were going to suffocate or something if we didn't get a Door open pretty quick. I should have known differently, if anybody should, because I'd once been in the Place without a Door for as long as a hundred sleeps during a foxhole stretch of the Change War and we'd had to start cycling our food and it had been okay.

And then, because it is also the way my mind works, I started to picture in a flash the consequences of our living together all by ourselves like Lili said.

I began to pair people off; I couldn't help it. Let's see, four women, six men, two ETs.

"Greta," I said, "you're going to be Miss Polly Andry for sure. We'll have a daily newspaper and folk-dancing classes, we'll shut the bar except evenings, Bruce'll keep a rhymed history of the Place."

I even thought, though I knew this part was strictly silly, about schools and children. I wondered what Siddy's would look like, or my little commandant's. "Don't go near the Void, dears." Of course that would be specially hard on the two ETs, but Sevensee at least wasn't so different and the genetics boys had made some wonderful advances and Maud ought to know about them and there were some amazing gadgets in Surgery when Doc sobered up. The patter of little hoofs...

"My fiance spoke to you about carrying a peace message to the rest of the cosmos," Lili added, "and bringing an end to the Big Change, and healing all the wounds that have been made in the Little Time."

I looked at Bruce. His face was set and strained, as will happen to the best of them when a girl starts talking about her man's business, and I don't know why, but I said to myself, "She's crucifying him, she's nailing him to his purpose as a woman will, even when there's not much point to it, as now."

And Lili went on, "It was a wonderful thought, but now we cannot carry or send any message and I believe it is too late in any event for a peace message to do any good. The cosmos is too raveled by change, too far gone. It will dissolve, fade, 'leave not a rack behind.' We're the survivors. The torch of existence has been put in our hands.

"We may already be all that's left in the cosmos, for have you thought that the Change Winds may have died at their source? We may never reach another cosmos, we may drift forever in the Void, but who of us has been Introverted before and who knows what we can or cannot do? We're a seed for a new future to grow from. Perhaps all doomed universes cast off seeds like this Place. It's a seed, it's an embryo, let it grow."

She looked swiftly at Bruce and then at Sid and she quoted, "'Come, my friends, 'tis not too late to seek a newer world'."

I squeezed Sid's hand and I started to say something to him, but he didn't know I was there; he was listening to Lili quote Tennyson with his eyes entranced and his mouth open, as if he were imagining new things to put into it—oh, Siddy!

And then I saw the others were looking at her the same way. Ilhilihis was seeing finer feather forests than long-dead Luna's grow. The greenhouse child Maud ap-Ares Davies was stowing away on a starship bound for another galaxy, or thinking how different her life might have been, the children she might have had, if she'd stayed on the planets and out of the Change World. Even Erich looked as though he might be blitzing new universes, and Mark subduing them, for an eight-legged *Führer-imperator*. Beau was throbbing up a wider Mississippi in a bigger-than-life sidewheeler.

Even I—well, I wasn't dreaming of a Greater Chicago. "Let's not go hog-wild on this sort of thing," I told myself, but I did look up at the Void and I got a shiver because I imagined it drawing away and the whole Place starting to grow.

"I truly meant what I said about a seed," Lili went on slowly. "I know, as you all do, that there are no children in the Change World, that there cannot be, that we all become instantly sterile, that what they call a curse is lifted from us girls and we are no longer in bondage to the moon."

She was right, all right—if there's one thing that's been proved a million times in the Change World, it's that.

"But we are no longer in the Change World," Lili said softly, "and its limitations should no longer apply to us, including that one. I feel deeply certain of it, but..." She looked around slowly. "...we are four women here and I thought one of us might have a surer indication."

My eyes followed hers around like anybody's would. In fact, everybody was looking around except Maud, and she had the silliest look of surprise on her face and it stayed there, and then, very carefully, she got down from the bar stool with her knitting. She looked at the half-finished pink bra with the long white needles stuck in it and her eyes bugged bigger yet, as if she were expecting it to turn into a baby sweater right then and there. Then she walked across the Place to Lili and stood beside her. While she was walking, the look of surprise changed to a quiet smile. The only other thing she did was throw her shoulders back a little.

I was jealous of her for a second, but it was a double miracle for her, considering her age, and I couldn't grudge her that. And to tell the truth, I was a little frightened, too. Even with Dave, I'd been bothered about this business of having babies.

Yet I stood up with Siddy—I couldn't stop myself and I guess he couldn't either—and hand in hand we walked to the control divan. Beau and Sevensee were there and Bruce, of course, and then, so help me, those Soldiers to the death, Kaby and Mark, started over from the bar and I couldn't see anything in their eyes about the greater glory of Crete and Rome, but something, I think, about each other, and after a moment Illy slowly detached himself from the piano and followed, lightly trailing his tentacles on the floor.

I couldn't exactly see him hoping for little Illies in this company, unless it was true what the jokes said about Lunans, but maybe he was being really disinterested and maybe he wasn't; maybe he was simply figuring that Illy ought to be on the side with the biggest battalions.

I heard dragging footsteps behind us and here came Doc from the Gallery, carrying in his folded arms an abstract sculpture as big as a newborn baby. It was an agglomeration of perfect shiny gray spheres the size of golf balls, shaping up to something like a large brain, but with holes showing through here and there. He held it out to us like an infant to be admired and worked his lips and tongue as if he were trying very hard to say something, though not a word came out that you could understand, and I thought, "Maxey Aleksevich may be speechless drunk and have all sorts of holes in his head, but he's got the right instincts, bless his soulful little Russian heart."

We were all crowded around the control divan like a football team huddling. The Peace Packers, it came to me. Sevensee would be fullback or center and Illy left end—what a receiver! The right number, too. Erich was alone at the bar, but now even he ("Oh, no, this can't be," I thought) came toward us. Then I saw that his face was working the worst ever. He stopped halfway and managed to force a smile, but it was the worst, too. "That's my little commandant," I thought, "no team spirit."

"So now Lili and Bruce—yes, and *Grossmutterchen* Maud—have their little nest," he said, and he wouldn't have had to push his voice very hard to get a screech. "But what are the rest of us supposed to be—cowbirds?"

He crooked his neck and flapped his hands and croaked, "Cuc-koo! Cuc-koo!" And I said to myself, "I often thought you were crazy, boy, but now I know."

"*Teufelsdreck!*—yes, Devil's dirt!—but you all seem to be infected with this dream of children. Can't you see that the Change World is the natural and proper end of evolution?—a period of enjoyment and measuring, an ultimate working out of things, which women call destruction—'Help, I'm being raped!' 'Oh, what are they doing to my children?'—but which men know as fulfillment.

"You're given good parts in *Götterdämmerung* and you go up to the author and tap him on the shoulder and say, 'Excuse me, Herr Wagner, but this Twilight of the Gods is just a bit morbid. Why don't you write an opera for me about the little ones, the dear little blue-eyed curly-tops? A plot? Oh, boy meets girl and they settle down to breed, something like that.'

"Devil's dirt doubled and damned! Have you thought what life will be like without a Door to go out of to find freedom and adventure, to measure your courage and keenness? Do you want to grow long gray beards hobbling around this asteroid turned inside out? Putter around indoors to the end of your days, mooning about little baby cosmoses?—incidentally, with a live bomb for company. The cave, the womb, the little gray home in the nest—is that what you want? It'll grow? Oh, yes, like the city engulfing the wild wood, a proliferation of *Kinder*, *Kirche*, *Küche*—I should live so long!

"Women!—how I hate their bright eyes as they look at me from the fireside, bent-shouldered, rocking, deeply happy to be old, and say, 'He's getting weak, he's giving out, soon I'll have to put him to bed and do the simplest things for him.' Your filthy Triple Goddess, Kaby, the birther, bride, and burier of man! Woman, the enfeebler, the fetterer, the crippler! Woman!—and the curly-headed little cancers she wants!"

He lurched toward us, pointing at Lili. "I never knew one who didn't want to cripple a man if you gave her the chance.

Cripple him, swaddle him, clip his wings, grind him to sausage to mold another man, hers, a doll man. You hid the Maintainer, you little smother-hen, so you could have your nest and your Brucie!"

He stopped, gasping, and I expected someone to bop him one on the schnozzle, and I think he did, too. I turned to Bruce and he was looking, I don't know how, sorry, guilty, anxious, angry, shaken, inspired, all at once, and I wished people sometimes had simple suburban reactions like magazine stories.

Then Erich made the mistake, if it was one, of turning toward Bruce and slowly staggering toward him, pawing the air with his hands as if he were going to collapse into his arms, and saying, "Don't let them get you, Bruce. Don't let them tie you down. Don't let them clip you—your words or your deeds. You're a Soldier. Even when you talked about a peace message, you talked about doing some smashing of your own. No matter what you think and feel, Bruce, no matter how much lying you do and how much you hide, you're really not on their side."

That did it.

It didn't come soon enough or, I think, in the right spirit to please me, but I will say it for Bruce that he didn't muck it up by tipping or softening his punch. He took one step forward and his shoulders spun and his fist connected sweet and clean.

As he did it, he said only one word, "Loki!" and darn if that didn't switch me back to a campfire in the Indiana Dunes and my mother telling me out of the Elder Saga about the malicious, sneering, all-spoiling Norse god and how, when the other gods came to trap him in his hideaway by the river, he was on the point of finishing knotting a mysterious net big enough, I had imagined, to snare the whole universe, and that if they'd come a minute later, he would have.

Erich was stretched on the floor, his head hitched up, rubbing his jaw and glaring at Bruce. Mark, who was standing beside me, moved a little and I thought he was going to do something, maybe even clobber Bruce in the old spirit of you can't do that to my buddy, but he just shook his head and said, "*Omnia vincit amor.*" I nudged him and said, "Meaning?" and he said, "Love licks everything."

I'd never have expected it from a Roman, but he was half right at any rate. Lili had her victory: Bruce clearing the field for the marriage by laying out the woman-hating boy friend who would be trying to get him to go out nights. At that moment, I think Bruce wanted Lili and a life with her more than he wanted to reform the Change World. Sure, us women have our little victories—until the legions come or the Little Corporal draws up his artillery or the Panzers roar down the road.

Erich scrambled to his feet and stood there in a half-slump, half-crouch, still rubbing his jaw and glaring at Bruce over his hand, but making no move to continue the fight, and I studied his face and said to myself, "If he can get a gun, he's going to shoot himself, I know."

Bruce started to say something and hesitated, like I would have in his shoes, and just then Doc got one of his unpredictable inspirations and went weaving out toward Erich, holding out the sculpture and making deaf-and-dumb noises like he had to us. Erich looked at him as if he were going to kill him, and then grabbed the sculpture and swung it up over his head and smashed it down on the floor, and for a wonder, it didn't shatter. It just skidded along in one piece and stopped inches from my feet.

That thing not breaking must have been the last straw for Erich. I swear I could see the red surge up through his eyes toward his brain. He swung around into the Stores sector and ran the few steps between him and the bronze bomb chest.

Everything got very slow motion for me, though I didn't do any moving. Almost every man started out after Erich. Bruce didn't, though, and Siddy turned back after the first surge forward, while Illy squunched down for a leap, and it was between Sevensee's hairy shanks and Beau's scissoring white pants that I saw that under-the-microscope circle of death's heads and watched Erich's finger go down on them in the order Kaby had given: one, three, five, six, two, four, seven. I was able to pray seven distinct times that he'd make a mistake.

He straightened up. Illy landed by the box like a huge silver spider and his tentacles whipped futilely across its top. The others surged to a frightened halt around them.

Erich's chest was heaving, but his voice was cool and collected as he said, "You mentioned something about our having a future, Miss Foster. Now you can make that more specific. Unless we get back to the cosmos and dump this box, or find a Spider A-tech, or manage to call headquarters for guidance on disarming the bomb, we have a future exactly thirty minutes long."

CHAPTER THIRTEEN
The Tiger is Loose

But whence he was, or of what wombe ybore, Of beasts, or of the earth, I have not red: But certes was with milke of wolves and tygres fed.
—*Spenser*

I guess when they really push the button or throw the switch or spring the trap or focus the beam or what have you, you don't faint or go crazy or anything else convenient. I didn't. Everything, everybody, every move that was made, every word that was spoken, was painfully real to me, like a hand twisting and squeezing things deep inside me, and I saw every least detail spotlighted and magnified like I had the seven skulls.

Erich was standing beyond the bomb chest; little smiles were ruffling his lips. I'd never seen him look so sharp. Illy was beside him, but not on his side, you understand. Mark, Sevensee and Beau were around the chest to the nearer side. Beau had dropped to a knee and was scanning the chest minutely, terror-under-control making him bend his head a little closer than he needed to for clear vision, but with his hands locked together behind his back, I guess to restrain the impulse to push any and everything that looked like a disarming button.

Doc was sprawled face down on the nearest couch, out like a light, I suppose.

Us four girls were still by the control divan. With Kaby, that surprised me, because she didn't look scared or frozen, but almost as intensely alive as Erich.

Sid had turned back, as I'd said, and had one hand stretched out toward but not touching the Minor Maintainer, and a look on his beardy face as if he were calling down death and destruction on every boozy rogue who had ever gone up from King's Lynn to Cambridge and London, and I realized why: if he'd thought of the Minor Maintainer a second sooner, he could have pinned Erich down with heavy gravity before he could touch the buttons.

Bruce was resting one hand on the head of the control divan and was looking toward the group around the chest, toward Erich, I think, as if Erich had done something rather wonderful for him, though I can't imagine myself being tickled at being included in anybody's suicide surprise party. Bruce looked altogether too dreamy, Brahma blast him, for someone who must have the same steel-spiked thought in his head that I know darn well the rest of us had: that in twenty-nine minutes or so, the Place would be a sun in a bag.

Erich was the first to get down to business, as I'd have laid any odds he would be. He had the jump on us and he wasn't going to lose it.

"Well, when are you going to start getting Lili to tell us where she hid the Maintainer? It has to be her—she was too certain it was gone forever when she talked. And Bruce must have seen from the bar who took the Maintainer, and who would he cover up for but his girl?"

There he was plagiarizing my ideas, but I guess I was willing to sign them over to him in full if he got us the right pail of water for that time-bomb.

He glanced at his wrist. "According to my Caller, you have twenty-nine and a half minutes, including the time it will take to get a Door or contact headquarters. When are you going to get busy on the girl?"

Bruce laughed a little—deprecatingly, so help me—and started toward him. "Look here, old man," he said, "there's no need to trouble Lili, or to fuss with headquarters, even if you could. Really not at all. Not to mention that your surmises are quite unfounded, old chap, and I'm a bit surprised at your advancing them. But that's quite all right because, as it happens, I'm an atomics technician and I even worked on that very bomb. To disarm it, you just have to fiddle a bit with some of the ankhs, those hoopy little crosses. Here, let me—"

Allah il allah, but it must have struck everybody as it did me as being just too incredible an assertion, too bloody British a bare-faced bluff, for Erich didn't have to say a word; Mark and Sevensee grabbed Bruce by the arms, one on each side, as he stooped toward the bronze chest, and they weren't gentle about it. Then Erich spoke.

"Oh, no, Bruce. Very sporting of you to try to cover up for your girl friend, but we aren't going to let ourselves be blown to stripped atoms twenty-eight minutes too soon while you monkey with the buttons, the very thing Benson-Carter warned against, and pray for a guesswork miracle. It's too thin, Bruce, when you come from 1917 and haven't been on the Big Time for a hundred sleeps and were calling for an A-tech yourself a few hours ago. Much too thin. Bruce, something is going to happen that I'm afraid you won't like, but you're going to have to put up with it. That is, unless Miss Foster decides to be cooperative."

"I say, you fellows, let me go," Bruce demanded, struggling experimentally. "I know it's a bit thick to swallow and I did give you the wrong impression calling for an A-tech, but I just wanted to capture your attention then; I didn't want to have to work on the bomb. Really, Erich, would they have ordered Benson-Carter to pick us up unless one of us were an A-tech? They'd be sure to include one in the bally operation."

"When they're using patchwork tactics?" Erich grinningly quoted back at him.

Kaby spoke up beside me and said, "Benson-Carter was a magician of matter and he was going on the operation disguised as an old woman. We have the cloak and hood with the other garments," and I wondered how this cold fish of a she-officer could be the same girl who was giving Mark slurpy looks not ten minutes ago.

"Well?" Erich asked, glancing at his Caller and then swinging his eyes around at us as if there must be some of the old *Wehrmacht* iron somewhere. We all found ourselves looking at Lili and she was looking so sharp herself, so ready to jump and so at bay, that it was all *I* needed, at any rate, to make Erich's theory about the Maintainer a rock-bottom certainty.

Bruce must have realized the way our minds were working, for he started to struggle in earnest and at the same time called, "For God's sake, don't do anything to Lili! Let me loose, you idiots! Everything's true I told you—I can save you from that bomb. Sevensee, you took my side against the Spiders; you've nothing to lose. Sid, you're an Englishman. Beau, you're a gentleman and you love her, too—for God's sake, stop them!"

Beau glanced up over his shoulder at Bruce and the others surging around close to his ankles and he had on his poker face. Sid I could tell was once more going through the purgatory of decision. Beau reached his own decision first and I'll say it for him that he acted on it fast and intelligently. Right from his kneeling position and before he'd even turned his head quite back, he jumped Erich.

But other things in this cosmos besides Man can pick sides and act fast. Illy landed on Beau midway and whipped his tentacles around him tight and they went wobbling around like a drunken white-and-silver barber pole. Beau got his hands each around a tentacle, and at the same time his face began to get purple, and I winced at what they were both going through.

Maybe Sevensee had a hoof in Sid's purgatory, because Bruce shook loose from the satyr and tried to knock out Mark, but the Roman twisted his arm and kept him from getting in a good punch.

Erich didn't make a move to mix into either fight, which is my little commandant all over. Using his fists on anybody but me is beneath him.

Then Sid made his choice, but there was no way for me to really tell what it was, for, as he reached for the Minor Maintainer, Kaby contemptuously snatched it away from his hands and gave him a knee in the belly that doubled me up in sympathy and sent him sprawling on his knees toward the fighters. On the return, Kaby gave Lili, who'd started to grab too, an effortless backhand smash that set her down on the divan.

Erich's face lit up like an electric sign and he kept his eyes fixed on Kaby.

She crouched a little, carrying her weight on the balls of her feet and firmly cradling the Minor Maintainer in her left arm, kind of like the captain of a basketball team planning an offensive. Then she waved her free hand decisively to the right. I didn't get it, but Erich did and Mark too, for Erich jumped for the Refresher sector and Mark let go of Bruce and followed him, ducking around Sevensee's arms, who was coming back into the fight on which side I don't know. Illy un-whipped from Beau and copied Erich and Mark with one big spring.

Then Kaby twisted a dial as far as it would go and Bruce, Beau, Sevensee and poor Siddy were slammed down and pinned to the floor by about eight gravities.

It should have been lighter near us—I hoped it was, but you couldn't tell from watching Siddy; he went flat on his face, spread-eagled, one hand stretched toward me so close, I could have touched it (but not let go!), and his mouth was open against the floor and he was gasping through a corner of it and I could see his spine trying to sink through his belly. Bruce just managed to get his head and one shoulder up a bit, and they all made me think of a Dore illustration of the *Inferno* where the cream of the damned are frozen up to their necks in ice in the innermost circle of Hell.

The gravity didn't catch me, although I could feel it in my left arm. I was mostly in the Refresher sector, but I dropped down flat too, partly out of a crazy compassion I have, but mostly because I didn't want to take a chance of having Kaby knock me down.

Erich, Mark and Illy had got clear and they headed toward us. Maud picked the moment to make her play; she hadn't much choice of times, if she wanted to make one. The Old Girl was looking it for once, but I guess the thought of her miracle must have survived alongside the fear of sacked sun and must have meant a lot to her, for she launched out fast, all set to straight-arm Kaby into the heavy gravity and grab the Minor Maintainer with the other hand.

CHAPTER FOURTEEN
"Now will You Talk?"

Like diamonds, we are cut with our own dust.
—Webster

Cretans have eyes under their back hair, or let's face it, Entertainers aren't Soldiers. Kaby weaved to one side and flicked a helpful hand and poor old Maud went where she'd been going to send Kaby. It sickened me to see the gravity take hold and yank her down.

I could have jumped up and made it four in a row for Kaby, but I'm not a bit brave when things like my life are at stake.

Lili was starting to get up, acting a little dazed. Kaby gently pushed her down again and quietly said, "Where is it?" and then hauled off and slapped her across the face. What got me was the matter-of-fact way Kaby did it. I can understand somebody getting mad and socking someone, or even deliberately working up a rage so as to be able to do something nasty, but this cold-blooded way turns my stomach.

Lili looked as if half her face were about to start bleeding, but she didn't look dazed any more and her jaw set. Kaby grabbed Lili's pearl necklace and twisted it around her neck and it broke and the pearls went bouncing around like ping-pong balls, so Kaby yanked down Lili's gray silk bandeau until it was around the neck and tightened that. Lili started to choke through her tight-pressed lips. Erich, Mark and Illy had come up and crowded around, but they seemed to be content with the job Kaby was doing.

"Listen, slut," she said, "we have no time. You have a healing room in this place. I can work the things."

"Here it comes," I thought, wishing I could faint. On top of everything, on top of death even, they had to drag in the nightmare personally stylized for me, the horror with my name on it. I wasn't going to be allowed to blow up peacefully. They weren't satisfied with an A-bomb. They had to write my private hell into the script.

"There is a thing called an Invertor," Kaby said exactly as I'd known she would, but as I didn't really hear it just then—a mental split I'll explain in a moment. "It opens you up so they can cure your insides without cutting your skin or making you bleed anywhere. It turns the big parts of you inside out, but not the blood tubes. All your skin—your eyes, ears, nose, toes, all of it—becoming the lining of a little hole that's half-filled with your hair.

"Meantime, your insides are exposed for whatever the healer wants to do to them. You live for a while on the air inside the hole. First the healer gives you an air that makes you sleep, or you go mad in about fifty heartbeats. We'll see what ten heartbeats do to you without the sleepy air. Now will you talk?"

I hadn't been listening to her, though, not the real me, or I'd have gone mad without getting the treatment. I once heard Doc say your liver is more mysterious and farther away from you than the stars, because although you live with your liver all your life, you never see it or learn to point to it instinctively, and the thought of someone messing around with that intimate yet unknown part of you is just too awful.

I knew I had to do something quick. Hell, at the first hint of Introversion, before Kaby had even named it, Illy had winced so that his tentacles were all drawn up like fat feather-sausages. Erich had looked at him questioningly, but that lousy Looney had un-endeared himself to me by squeaking, "Don't mind me, I'm just sensitive. Get on with the girl. Make her tell."

Yes, I knew I had to do something, and here on the floor that meant thinking hard and in high gear about something else. The screwball sculpture Erich had tried to smash was a foot from my nose and I saw a faint trail of white stuff where it had skidded. I reached out and touched the trail; it was finely gritty, like powdered glass. I tipped up the sculpture and the part on which it had skidded wasn't marred at all, not even dulled; the gray spheres were as glisteningly bright as ever. So I knew the trail was diamond dust rubbed off the diamonds in the floor by something even harder.

That told me the sculpture was something special and maybe Doc had had a real idea in his pickled brain when he'd been pushing the thing at all of us and trying to tell us something. He hadn't managed to say anything then, but he had earlier when he'd been going to tell us what to do about the bomb, and maybe there was a connection.

I twisted my memory hard and let it spring back and I got "Inversh...bosh..." Bosh, indeed! Bosh and inverse bosh to all boozers, Russki or otherwise.

So I quick tried the memory trick again and this time I got "glovsh" and then I grasped and almost sneezed on diamond dust as I watched the pieces fit themselves together in my mind like a speeded-up movie reel.

It all hung on that black right-hand hussar's glove Lili had produced for Bruce. Only she couldn't have found it in Stores, because we'd searched every fractional pigeonhole later on and there hadn't been any gloves there, not even the left-hand mate there would have been. Also, Bruce had had two left-hand gloves to start with, and we had been through the whole Place with a fine-tooth comb, and there had been only the two black gloves on the floor where Bruce had kicked them off the bar—those two and those two only, the left-hand glove he'd brought from outside and the right-hand glove Lili had produced for him.

So a left-hand glove had disappeared—the last I'd seen of it, Lili had been putting it on her tray—and a right-hand glove had appeared. Which could only add up to one thing: Lili had turned the left-hand glove into an identical right. She couldn't have done it by turning it inside out the ordinary way, because the lining was different.

But as I knew only too sickeningly well, there was an extraordinary way to turn things inside out, things like human beings. You merely had to put them on the Invertor in Surgery and flick the switch for full Inversion.

Or you could flick it for partial Inversion and turn something into a perfect three-dimensional mirror image of itself, just what a right-hand glove is of a left. Rotation through the fourth dimension, the science boys call it; I've heard of it being used in surgery on the highly asymmetric Martians, and even to give a socially impeccable right hand to a man who'd lost one, by turning an amputated right arm into an amputated left.

Ordinarily, nothing but live things are ever Inverted in Surgery and you wouldn't think of doing it to an inanimate object, especially in a Place where the Doc's a drunk and the Surgery hasn't been used for hundreds of sleeps.

But when you've just fallen in love, you think of wonderful crazy things to do for people. Drunk with love, Lili had taken Bruce's extra left-hand glove into Surgery, partially Inverted it, and got a right-hand glove to give him.

What Doc had been attempting to say with his "Inversh…bosh…" was "Invert the box," meaning we should put the bronze chest through full Inversion to get at the bomb inside to disarm it. Doc too had got the idea from Lili's trick with the glove. What an inside-out tactical atomic bomb would look like, I could not imagine and did not particularly care to see. I might have to, though, I realized.

But the fast-motion film was still running in my head. Later on, Lili had decided like I had that her lover was going to lose out in his plea for mutiny unless she could give him a really captive audience—and maybe, even then, she had been figuring on creating the nest for Bruce's chicks and...all those other things we'd believed in for a while. So she'd taken the Major Maintainer and remembered the glove, and not many seconds later, she had set down on a shelf of the Art Gallery an object that no one would think of questioning—except someone who knew the Gallery by heart.

I looked at the abstract sculpture a foot from my nose, at the clustered gray spheres the size of golf balls. I had known that the inside of the Maintainer was made up of vastly tough, vastly hard giant molecules, but I hadn't realized they were quite *that* big.

I said to myself, "Greta, this is going to give you a major psychosis, but you're the one who has to do it, because no one is going to listen to your deductions when they're all practically living on negative time already."

I got up as quietly as if I were getting out of a bed I shouldn't have been in—there are some things Entertainers are good at—and Kaby was just saying "you go mad in about fifty heartbeats." Everybody on their feet was looking at Lili. Sid seemed to have moved, but I had no time for him except to hope he hadn't done anything that might attract attention to me.

I stepped out of my shoes and walked rapidly to Surgery— there's one good thing about this hardest floor anywhere, it doesn't creak. I walked through the Surgery screen that is like a wall of opaque, odorless cigarette smoke and I concentrated on remembering my snafued nurse's training, and before I had time to panic, I had the sculpture positioned on the gleaming table of the Invertor.

I froze for a moment when I reached for the Inversion switch, thinking of the other time and trying to remember what it had been that bothered me so much about an inside-out brain being bigger and not having eyes, but then I either thumbed my nose at my nightmare or kissed my sanity good-by, I don't know which, and twisted the switch all the way over, and there was the Major Maintainer winking blue about three times a second as nice as you could want it.

It must have been working as sweet and steady as ever, all the time it was Inverted, except that, being inside out, it had hocused the direction finders.

CHAPTER FIFTEEN
Lord Spider

...black legged spiders with red hearts of hell.
—marquis

"Jesu!" I turned and Sid's face was sticking through the screen like a tinted bas-relief hanging on a gray wall and I got the impression he had peered unexpectedly through a slit in an arras into Queen Elizabeth's bedroom.

He didn't have any time to linger on the sensation, even if he'd wanted to, for an elbow with a copper band thrust through the screen and dug his ribs and Kaby marched Lili in by the neck. Erich, Mark and Illy were right behind. They caught the blue flashes and stopped dead, staring at the long-lost. Erich spared me one look which seemed to say, so you did it, not that it matters. Then he stepped forward and picked it up and held it solidly to his left side in the double right-angle made by fingers, forearm and chest, and reached for the Introversion switch with a look on his face as if he were opening a fifth of whisky.

The blue light died and Change Winds hit me like a stiff drink that had been a long, long time in coming, like a hot trumpet note out of nowhere.

I felt the changing pasts blowing through me, and the uncertainties whistling past, and ice-stiff reality softening with all its duties and necessities, and the little memories shredding away and dancing off like autumn leaves, leaving maybe not even ghosts behind, and all the crazy moods like Mardi Gras dancers pouring down an evening street, and something inside me had the nerve to say it didn't care whether Greta Forzane's death was riding in those Winds because they felt so good.

I could tell it was hitting the others the same way. Even battered, tight-lipped Lili seemed to be saying, you're making me drink the stuff and I hate you for it, but I do love it. I guess we'd all had the worry that even finding and Extroverting the Maintainer wouldn't put us back in touch with the cosmos and give us those Winds we hate and love.

The thing that cut through to us as we stood there glowing was not the thought of the bomb, though that would have come in a few seconds more, but Sid's voice. He was still standing in the screen, except that now his face was out the other side and we could just see parts of his gray-doubleted back, but, of course, his "Jesu!" came through the screen as if it weren't there.

At first I couldn't figure out who he could be talking to, but I swear I never heard his voice so courtly obsequious before, so strong and yet so filled with awe and an under-note of, yes, sheer terror.

"Lord, I am filled from top to toe with confusion that you should so honor my poor Place," he said. "Poor say I and mine, when I mean that I have ever busked it faithfully for you, not dreaming that you would ever condescend…yet knowing that your eye was certes ever upon me…though I am but as a poor pinch of dust adrift between the suns…I abase myself. Prithee, how may I serve thee, sir? I know not e'en how most suitably to address thee, Lord… King… Emperor Spider!"

I felt like I was getting very small, but not a bit less visible, worse luck, and even with the Change Winds inside me to give me courage, I thought this was really too much, coming on top of everything else; it was simply unfair.

At the same time, I realized it was to be expected that the big bosses would have been watching us with their unblinking beady black eyes ever since we had Introverted waiting to pounce if we should ever come out of it. I tried to picture what was on the other side of the screen and I didn't like the assignment.

But in spite of being petrified, I had a hard time not giggling, like the zany at graduation exercises, at the way the other ones in Surgery were taking it.

I mean the Soldiers. They each stiffened up like they had the old ramrod inside them, and their faces got that important look, and they glanced at each other and the floor without lowering their heads, as if they were measuring the distance between their feet and mentally chalking alternate sets of footprints to step into. The way Erich and Kaby held the Major and Minor Maintainers became formal; the way they checked their Callers and nodded reassuringly was positively esoteric. Even Illy somehow managed to look as if he were on parade.

Then from beyond the screen came what was, under the circumstances, the worst noise I've ever heard, a seemingly wordless distant-sounding howling and wailing, with a note of menace that made me shake, although it also had a nasty familiarity about it I couldn't place. Sid's voice broke into it, loud, fast and frightened.

"Your pardon, Lord, I did not think…certes, the gravity… I'll attend to it on the instant." He whipped a hand and half a head back through the screen, but without looking back and snapped his fingers, and before I could blink, Kaby had put the Minor Maintainer in his hand.

Sid went completely out of sight then and the howling stopped, and I thought that if that was the way a Lord Spider expressed his annoyance at being subjected to incorrect gravity, I hoped the bosses wouldn't start any conversations with me.

Erich pursed his lips and threw the other Soldiers a nod and the four of them marched through the screen as if they'd drilled a lifetime for this moment. I had the wild idea that Erich might give me his arm, but he strode past me as if I were…an Entertainer.

I hesitated a moment then, but I had to see what was happening outside, even if I got eaten up for it. Besides, I had a bit of the thought that if these formalities went on much longer, even a Lord Spider was going to discover just how immune he was to confined atomic blast.

I walked through the screen with Lili beside me.

The Soldiers had stopped a few feet in front of it. I looked around ahead for whatever it was going to turn out to be, prepared to drop a curtsy or whatever else, bar nothing, that seemed expected of me.

I had a hard time spotting the beast. Some of the others seemed to be having trouble too. I saw Doc weaving around foolishly by the control divan, and Bruce and Beau and Sevensee and Maud on their feet beyond it, and I wondered whether we were dealing with an invisible monster; ought to be easy enough for the bosses to turn a simple trick like invisibility.

Then I looked sharply left where everyone else, even glassy-eyed Doc, was coming to look, into the Door sector, only there wasn't any monster there or even a Door, but just Siddy holding the Minor Maintainer and grinning like when he is threatening to tickle me, only more fiendishly.

"Not a move, masters," he cried, his eyes dancing, "or I'll pin the pack of you down, marry and amen I will. It is my firm purpose to see the Place blasted before I let this instrument out of my hands again."

My first thought was, "'Sblood but Siddy is a real actor! I don't care if he didn't study under anyone later than Burbage, that just proves how good Burbage is."

Sid had convinced us not only that the real Spiders had arrived, but earlier that the gravity in the edge of Stores had been a lot heavier than it actually was. He completely fooled all those Soldiers, including my swelled-headed victorious little commandant, and I kind of filed away the timing of that business of reaching out the hand and snapping the fingers without looking, it was so good.

"Beauregard!" Sid called. "Get to the Major Maintainer and call headquarters. But don't come through Door, marry go by Refresher. I'll not trust a single Demon of you in this sector with me until much more has been shown and settled."

"Siddy, you're wonderful," I said, starting toward him. "As soon as I got the Maintainer unsnarled and looked around and saw your sweet old face—"

"Back, tricksy trull! Not the breadth of one scarlet toenail nearer me, you Queen of Sleights and High Priestess of Deception!" he bellowed. "You least of all do I trust. Why you hid the Maintainer, I know not, 'faith, but later you'll discover the truth to me or I'll have your gizzard."

I could see there was going to have to be a little explaining.

Doc, touched off, I guess, by Sid waving his hand at me, threw back his head and let off one of those shuddery Siberian wolf-howls he does so blamed well. Sid waved toward him sharply and he shut up, beaming toothily, but at least I knew who was responsible for the Spider wail of displeasure that Sid had either called for or more likely got as a gift of the gods and used in his act.

Beau came circling around fast and Erich shoved the Major Maintainer into his hands without making any fuss. The four Soldiers were looking pretty glum after losing their grand review.

Beau dumped some junk off one of the Art Gallery's sturdy taborets and set the Major Maintainer on it carefully but fast, and quickly knelt in front of it and whipped on some earphones and started to tune. The way he did it snatched away from me my inward glory at my big Inversion brainwave so fast, I might never have had it, and there was nothing in my mind again but the bronze bomb chest.

I wondered if I should suggest Inverting the thing, but I said to myself, "Uh-uh, Greta, you got no diploma to show them and there probably isn't time to try two things, anyway."

Then Erich for once did something I wanted him to, though I didn't care for its effect on my nerves, by looking at his Caller and saying quietly, "Nine minutes to go, if Place time and cosmic time are synching."

Beau was steady as a rock and working adjustments so fine that I couldn't even see his fingers move.

Then, at the other end of the Place, Bruce took a few steps toward us. Sevensee and Maud followed a bit behind him. I remembered Bruce was another of our nuts with a private program for blowing up the place.

"Sidney," he called, and then, when he'd got Sid's attention, "Remember, Sidney, you and I both came down to London from Peterhouse."

I didn't get it. Then Bruce looked toward Erich with a devil-may-care challenge and toward Lili as if he were asking her forgiveness for something. I couldn't read her expression; the bruises were blue on her throat and her cheek was puffy.

Then Bruce once more shot Erich that look of challenge and he spun and grabbed Sevensee by a wrist and stuck out a foot—even half-horses aren't too sharp about infighting, I guess, and the satyr had every right to feel at least as confused as I felt—and sent him stumbling into Maud, and the two of them tumbled to the floor in a jumble of hairy legs and pearl-gray frock. Bruce raced to the bomb chest.

Most of us yelled, "Stop him, Sid, pin him down," or something like that—I know I did because I was suddenly sure that he'd been asking Lili's pardon for blowing the two of them up—and all the rest of us too, the love-blinded stinker.

Sid had been watching him all the time and now he lifted his hand to the Minor Maintainer, but then he didn't touch any of the dials, just watched and waited, and I thought, "Shaitan shave us! Does Siddy want in on death, too? Ain't he satisfied with all he knows about life?"

Bruce had knelt and was twisting some things on the front of the chest, and it was all as bright as if he were under a bank of Klieg lights, and I was telling myself I wouldn't know anything when the fireball fired, and not believing it, and Sevensee and Maud had got unscrambled and were starting for Bruce, and the rest of us were yelling at Sid, except that Erich was just looking at Bruce very happily, and Sid was still not doing anything, and it was unbearable except just then I felt the little arteries start to burst in my brain like a string of fire-crackers and the old aorta pop, and for good measure, a couple of valves come unhinged in my ticker, and I was thinking, "Well, now I know what it's like to die of heart failure and high blood pressure," and having a last quiet smile at having cheated the bomb, when Bruce jumped up and back from the chest.

"That does it!" he announced cheerily. "She's as safe as the Bank of England."

Sevensee and Maud stopped themselves just short of knocking him down and I said to myself, "Hey, let's get a move on! I thought heart attacks were fast."

Before anyone else could speak, Beau did. He had turned around from the Major Maintainer and pulled aside one of the earphones.

"I got headquarters," he said crisply. "They told me how to disarm the bomb—I merely said I thought we ought to know. What did you do, sir?" he called to Bruce.

"There's a row of four ankhs just below the lock. The first to your left you give a quarter turn to the right, the second a quarter turn to the left, same for the fourth, and you don't touch the third."

"That is it, sir," Beau confirmed.

The long silence was too much for me; I guess I must have the shortest span for unspoken relief going. I drew some nourishment out of my restored arteries into my brain cells and yelled, "Siddy, I know I'm a tricksy trull and the High Vixen of all Foxes, but what the Hell is Peterhouse?"

"The oldest college at Cambridge," he told me rather coolly.

CHAPTER SIXTEEN
The Possibility-Binders

"Familiar with infinite universe sheafs and open-ended postulate systems?—the notion that everything is possible—and I mean everything—and everything has happened. Everything."
—Heinlein

An hour later, I was nursing a weak highball and a black eye in the sleepy-time darkness on the couch farthest from the piano, half watching the highlighted party going on around it and the bar, while the Place waited for rendezvous with Egypt and the Battle of Alexandria.

Sid had swept all our outstanding problems into one big bundle and, since his hand held the joker of the Minor Maintainer, he had settled them all as high-handedly as if they'd been those of a bunch of schoolkids.

It amounted to this:

We'd been Introverted when most of the damning things had happened, so presumably only we knew about them, and we were all in so deep one way or another that we'd all have to keep quiet to protect our delicate complexions.

Well, Erich's triggering the bomb did balance rather neatly Bruce's incitement to mutiny, and there was Doc's drinking, while everybody who had declared for the peace message had something to hide. Mark and Kaby I felt inclined to trust anywhere, Maud for sure, and Erich in this particular matter, damn him. Illy I didn't feel at all easy about, but I told myself there always has to be a fly in the ointment—a darn big one this time, and furry.

Sid didn't mention his own dirty linen, but he knew we knew he'd flopped badly as boss of the Place and only recouped himself by that last-minute flimflam.

Remembering Sid's trick made me think for a moment about the real Spiders. Just before I snuck out of Surgery, I'd had a vivid picture of what they must look like, but now I couldn't get it again. It depressed me, not being able to remember—oh, I probably just imagined I'd had a picture, like a hophead on a secret-of-the-universe kick. Me ever find out anything about the Spiders?—except for nervous notions like I'd had during the recent fracas?—what a laugh!

The funniest thing (ha-ha!) was that I had ended up the least-trusted person. Sid wouldn't give me time to explain how I'd deduced what had happened to the Maintainer, and even when Lili spoke up and admitted hiding it, she acted so bored I don't think everybody believed her—although she did spill the realistic detail that she hadn't used partial Inversion on the glove; she'd just turned it inside out to make it a right and then done a full Inversion to get the lining back inside.

I tried to get Doc to confirm that he'd reasoned the thing out the same way I had, but he said he had been blacked out the whole time, except during the first part of the hunt, and he didn't remember having any bright ideas at all. Right now, he was having Maud explain to him twice, in detail, everything that had happened. I decided that it was going to take a little more work before my reputation as a great detective was established.

I looked over the edge of the couch and just made out in the gloom one of Bruce's black gloves. It must have been kicked there. I fished it up. It was the right-hand one. My big clue, and was I sick of it! Got mittens, God forbid! I slung it away and, like a lurking octopus, Illy shot up a tentacle from the next couch, where I hadn't known he was resting, and snatched the glove like it was a morsel of underwater garbage. These ETs can seem pretty shuddery non-human at times.

I thought of what a cold-blooded, skin-saving louse Illy had been, and about Sid and his easy suspicions, and Erich and my black eye, and how, as usual, I'd got left alone in the end. My men!

Bruce had explained about being an A-tech. Like a lot of us, he'd had several widely different jobs during his first weeks in the Change World and one of them had been as secretary to a group of the minor atomics boys from the Manhattan-Project-Earth-Satellite days. I gathered he'd also absorbed some of his bothersome ideas from them. I hadn't quite decided yet what species of heroic heel he belonged to, but he was thick with Mark and Erich again. Everybody's men!

Sid didn't have to argue with anybody; all the wild compulsions and mighty resolves were dead now, anyway until they'd had a good long rest. I sure could use one myself, I knew.

The party at the piano was getting wilder. Lili had been dancing the black bottom on top of it and now she jumped down into Sid's and Sevensee's arms, taking a long time about it. She'd been drinking a lot and her little gray dress looked about as innocent on her as diapers would on Nell Gwyn. She continued her dance, distributing her marks of favor equally between Sid, Erich and the satyr. Beau didn't mind a bit, but serenely pounded out "Tonight's the Night," which she'd practically shouted to him not two minutes ago.

I was glad to be out of the party. Who can compete with a highly experienced, utterly disillusioned seventeen-year-old really throwing herself away for the first time?

Something touched my hand. Illy had stretched a tentacle into a furry wire to return me the black glove, although he ought to have known I didn't want it. I pushed it away, privately calling Illy a washed-out moronic tarantula, and right away I felt a little guilty. What right had I to be critical of Illy? Would my own character have shown to advantage if I'd been locked in with eleven octopoids a billion years away? For that matter, where did I get off being critical of anyone?

Still, I was glad to be out of the party, though I kept on watching it. Bruce was drinking alone at the bar. Once Sid had gone over to him and they'd had one together and I'd heard Bruce reciting from Rupert Brooke those deliberately corny lines, "For England's the one land, I know, Where men with Splendid Hearts may go; and Cambridgeshire, of all England, The Shire for Men who Understand;" and I'd remembered that Brooke too had died young in World War One and my ideas had got fuzzy. But mostly Bruce was just calmly drinking by himself. Every once in a while Lili would look at him and stop dead in her dancing and laugh.

I'd figured out this Bruce-Lili-Erich business as well as I cared to. Lili had wanted the nest with all her heart and nothing else would ever satisfy her, and now she'd go to hell her own way and probably die of Bright's disease for a third time in the Change World. Bruce hadn't wanted the nest or Lili as much as he wanted the Change World and the chances it gave for Soldierly cavorting and poetic drunks; Lili's seed wasn't his idea of healing the cosmos; maybe he'd make a real mutiny some day, but more likely he'd stick to bar-room epics.

His and Lili's infatuation wouldn't die completely, no matter how rancid it looked right now. The real-love angle might go, but Change would magnify the romance angle and it might seem to them like a big thing of a sort if they met again.

Erich had his *Kamerad*, shaped to suit him, who'd had the guts and cleverness to disarm the bomb he'd had the guts to trigger. You have to hand it to Erich for having the nerve to put us all in a situation where we'd have to find the Maintainer or fry, but I don't know anything disgusting enough to hand to him.

I had tried a while back. I had gone up behind him and said, "Hey, how's my wicked little commandant? Forgotten your *und so weiter?*" and as he turned, I clawed my nails and slammed him across the cheek. That's how I got the black eye. Maud wanted to put an electronic leech on it, but I took the old handkerchief in ice water. Well, at any rate Erich had his scratches to match Bruce's, not as deep, but four of them, and I told myself maybe they'd get infected—I hadn't washed my hands since the hunt. Not that Erich doesn't love scars.

Mark was the one who helped me up after Erich knocked me down.

"You got any omnias for that?" I snapped at him.

"For what?" Mark asked.

"Oh, for everything that's been happening to us," I told him disgustedly.

He seemed to actually think for a moment and then he said, "*Omnia mutantur, nihil interit.*"

"Meaning?" I asked him.

He said, "All things change, but nothing is really lost."

It would be a wonderful philosophy to stand with against the Change Winds. Also damn silly. I wondered if Mark really believed it. I wished I could. Sometimes I come close to thinking it's a lot of baloney trying to be any decent kind of Demon, even a good Entertainer. Then I tell myself, "That's life, Greta. You've got to love through it somehow." But there are times when some of these cookies are not too easy to love.

Something brushed the palm of my hand again. It was Illy's tentacle, with the tendrils of the tip spread out like a little bush. I started to pull my hand away, but then I realized the Loon was simply lonely. I surrendered my hand to the patterned gossamer pressures of feather-talk.

Right away I got the words, "Feeling lonely, Greta girl?"

It almost floored me, I tell you. Here I was understanding feather-talk, which I just didn't, and I was understanding it in English, which didn't make sense at all.

For a second, I thought Illy must have spoken, but I knew he hadn't, and for a couple more seconds I thought he was working telepathy on me, using the feather-talk as cues. Then I tumbled to what was happening: he was playing English on my palm like on the keyboard of his squeakbox, and since I could play English on a squeakbox myself, my mind translated automatically.

Realizing this almost gave my mind stage fright, but I was too fagged to be hocused by self-consciousness. I just lay back and let the thoughts come through. It's good to have someone talk to you, even an underweight octopus, and without the squeaks Illy didn't sound so silly; his phrasing was soberer.

"Feeling sad, Greta girl, because you'll never understand what's happening to us all," Illy asked me, "because you'll never be anything but a shadow fighting shadows—and trying to love shadows in between the battles? It's time you understood we're not really fighting a war at all, although it looks that way, but going through a kind of evolution, though not exactly the kind Erich had in mind.

"Your Terran thought has a word for it and a theory for it—a theory that recurs on many worlds. It's about the four orders of life: Plants, Animals, Men and Demons. Plants are energy-binders—they can't move through space or time, but they can clutch energy and transform it. Animals are space-binders—they can move through space. Man (Terran or ET, Lunan or non-Lunan) is a time-binder—he has memory.

"Demons are the fourth order of evolution, possibility-binders—they can make all of what might be part of what is, and that is their evolutionary function. Resurrection is like the metamorphosis of a caterpillar into a butterfly: a third-order being breaks out of the chrysalis of its lifeline into fourth-order life. The leap from the ripped cocoon of an unchanging reality is like the first animal's leap when he ceases to be a plant, and the Change World is the core of meaning behind the many myths of immortality.

"All evolution looks like a war at first—octopoids against monopoids, mammals against reptiles. And it has a necessary dialectic: there must be the thesis—we call it Snake—and the antithesis—Spider—before there's the ultimate synthesis, when all possibilities are fully realized in one ultimate universe. The Change War isn't the blind destruction it seems.

"Remember that the Serpent is your symbol of wisdom and the Spider your sign for patience. The two names are rightly frightening to you, for all high existence is a mixture of horror and delight. And don't be surprised, Greta girl, at the range of my words and thoughts; in a way, I've had a billion years to study Terra and learn her languages and myths.

"Who are the real Spiders and Snakes, meaning who were the first possibility-binders? Who was Adam, Greta girl? Who was Cain? Who were Eve and Lilith?

"In binding all possibility, the Demons also bind the mental with the material. All fourth-order beings live inside and outside all minds, throughout the whole cosmos. Even this Place is, after its fashion, a giant brain: its floor is the brainpan, the boundary of the Void is the cortex of gray matter—yes, even the Major and Minor Maintainers are analogues of the pineal and pituitary glands, which in some form sustain all nervous systems.

"There's the real picture, Greta girl."

The feather-talk faded out and Illy's tendril tips merged into a soft pad on which I fingered, "Thanks, Daddy Longlegs."

Chewing over in my mind what Illy had just told me, I looked back at the gang around the piano. The party seemed to be breaking up; at least some of them were chopping away at it. Sid had gone to the control divan and was getting set to tune in Egypt. Mark and Kaby were there with him, bursting with eagerness and the vision of tanks on ranks of mounted Zombie bowmen going up in a mushroom cloud; I thought of what Illy had told me and I managed a smile—seems we've got to win and lose all the battles, every which way.

Mark had just put on his Parthian costume, groaning cheerfully, "Trousers again!" and was striding around under a hat like a fur-lined ice-cream cone and with the sleeves of his metal-stuffed candys flapping over his hands. He waved a short sword with a heart-shaped guard at Bruce and Erich and told them to get a move on.

Kaby was going along on the operation wearing the old-woman disguise intended for Benson-Carter. I got a half-hearted kick out of knowing she was going to have to cover that chest and hobble.

Bruce and Erich weren't taking orders from Mark just yet. Erich went over and said something to Bruce at the bar, and Bruce got down and went over with Erich to the piano, and Erich tapped Beau on the shoulder and leaned over and said something to him, and Beau nodded and yanked "Limehouse Blues" to a fast close and started another piece, something slow and nostalgic.

Erich and Bruce waved to Mark and smiled, as if to show him that whether he came over and stood with them or not, the legate and the lieutenant and the commandant were very much together. And while Sevensee hugged Lili with a simple enthusiasm that made me wonder why I've wasted so much imagination on genetic treatments for him, Erich and Bruce sang:

"To the legion of the lost ones, to the cohort of the damned, To our brothers in the tunnels outside time, Sing three Change-resistant Zombies, raised from death and robot-crammed, And Commandos of the Spiders— Here's to crime! We're three blind mice on the wrong time-track, Hush—hush—hush! We've lost our now and will never get back, Hush—hush—hush! Change Commandos out on the spree, Damned through all possibility, Ghostgirls, think kindly on such as we, Hush—hush—hush!"

While they were singing, I looked down at my charcoal skirt and over at Maud and Lili and I thought, "Three gray hustlers for three black hussars, that's our speed." Well, I'd never thought of myself as a high-speed job, winning all the races—I wouldn't feel comfortable that way. Come to think of it, we've got to lose and win all the races in the long run, the way the course is laid out.

I fingered to Illy, "That's the picture, all right, Spider boy."

THE END